D1069389

"There's so much genius in this book that I couldn't capture it in a sentence or two. It's a WINNER!!!

The story is inspiring and empowering, showing how each of us has strayed from our spiritual origin and roots and how we can once again re-unite with our higher purpose. There's so much wisdom, charm, and healing packed into this little book. I couldn't put it down."

Dr. Scott and Shannon Peck, authors, *Love Skills for Personal & Global Transformation*

"Jeanne Webster spins a little of her own spider magic with a fable that is well on its way to being a modern classic. Listen quietly as the compassionate voice of Creator speaks through a treasure-trove of divine encounters with our majestic animal brethren and a lively cast of entertaining characters. Strays reminds us that the hero's journey is our birthright and always within our grasp, if only we listen to the gentle wisdom of nature. It is a journey that you can embark upon, right now, by reading this enlightening book. If you're a seeker of spiritual truth and Divine wisdom, you'll find what you're looking for in Strays."

Michael R. Smith, Ph.D., author of *Navigating 2012: Thriving in Earth's New Age*

"Jeanne Webster has made some core life truths fun, engaging and easy to digest. You'll love reading this book and it could change your life."

Chris Attwood, Co-author of the NY Times bestseller, *The Passion Test - The Effortless Path to Discovering Your Life Purpose*

"One of the best books I have ever read! Waiting on the sequel! I fell in love with Max." ~ Lori- Murphy - North Carolina

"I bought my neighbor's book and I absolutely loved it. It reminded me of another book I recently read, *The Shack* - but with one exception, I like Webster's novel better. She is a gifted and skilled writer with an ability to carry her reader effortlessly along the path of this inspirational journey." ~Carol M.

"I love your book Strays. My husband and I were visiting the town of Helen, Georgia in October when your husband came up to me and asked me if I liked to read. I told him yes; if it was good clean reading. He assured me I would enjoy this book. So I purchased your book. I laughed, I cried, and I could not put your book down until I finished reading it. Now I am waiting on the sequel to be finished…so hurry!"~ Barbara A. Dupree - Coushatta, Louisiana

"I could not put this book down! What an amazing story. On a scale from 1 to 10 I would rate it a 15. I'm going to read it for the second time now and I know I will enjoy it as much, if not more, than the first time I read it." ~ Linda Gavel - Asheville, North Carolina

"The best book I've read in ten years! Thank you for being inspired and writing this inspiration for so many people including myself. May you continue on your path and lead others to finding theirs." ~ Rosemary Dixson

"Thank you so much for this book! I read it through in a couple of days and decided just to start over. I'm moving slower through Strays this time and taking the time to read over the passages and letting the words really sink in. I can't tell you how much I loved it!" ~ Greg T.

Strays

Jeanne Webster

PERSONHOOD PRESS
Fawnskin, California

STRAYS

Personhood Press
PO Box 370
Fawnskin, CA 92333
T: (909) 866-2912   F: (909) 866-2961
Orders: (800) 429-1192
www.personhoodpress.com
info@personhoodpress.com

ISBN: 9781932181845
Library of Congress Control Number:
2010939782

Book Website: www.straysthebook.com

PRINTED IN THE UNITED STATES OF AMERICA
Cover Design by: Lea Venturo
Our Cover Dog, Cooper the Golden Retriever
Cooper is a rescue from the Humane Society of Atlanta, now living a wonderful life in his forever home.

To all the storytellers of the oral tradition who keep Earth wisdom alive and available to anyone with the ears to hear it.

***

The stories in this book are stories I heard either as a child or in my adult years. They have been handed down from generation to generation and told from the back seat of cars, around the fire at pow wows or in the living rooms of mountain grandmothers. Only one or two stories were written by me in keeping with the theme of the book.

Before there was the written word, stories served as education. They taught us about life and how to live it with purpose and meaning. These stories taught us morals and values. They entertained, terrified and sparked the imaginations of the listeners. Anyone who ever sat around a crackling fire, caught up in the spell a good storyteller weaves, knows the simple power of the spoken word.

It is my great pleasure to bring these stories back to you. Wrapped in the larger story, they have the opportunity to live again in your imagination.

Acknowledgments

There is a special bond that takes place between the author of a book and the reader. It's the end result and what writers dream of when and if they sleep. And as any author knows, before that bond can be created, there are countless others whose names never appear on the cover who make a book possible. I would like to acknowledge those people in my life whose fingerprints are all over this book.

—First and always, to my children, Sara and Nick. They know me and my flaws and love me anyway. My husband Claude, whose support and enthusiasm keep me and our home running smoothly. And our four-legged companions Usdii and Jake, who protect, guide, guard, love and remind us daily of the wonder and wisdom of the natural world.

—My editor Londa who became my dear friend and who worked on this manuscript countless more hours than required. Without her keen eyes and open heart, this book wouldn't have been nearly as much fun to write or edit…and edit…and edit.

—To Kathy Glass who polished, without changing my voice.

—To Rabun Animal Hospital for all their advice on snakes, snake bite and various illnesses and treatments. Thanks for being so willing to help.

—To Rita, Dan, Floss and Grandma Barbara, my beta readers for their eyes on the content of the book. Your input was priceless.

—To Janice Phelps Williams for the initial cover concept and Lea Venturo for the graphics and design. Much of the time, a book is judged by its cover.

—To the Uppercase Literary Source, a group of published divas. Our weekly meetings must have Robert and his Rules of Order tossing in his grave.

—And last, but hardly least, to Cathy and Bradley, my publishers, for shepherding *Strays* so lovingly and joyfully. There are hardly words to tell you how much I appreciate and enjoy our partnership.

But ask now the beasts,
And they will teach you;
And the birds of the air,
And they will tell you;
Or speak to the earth,
And it will teach you;
And the fishes of the sea
Will explain to you

-Job 12:7-8
KJV

ONE

Silk...who would wear silk in the rain?

Lying on the wet steps, Jane had no idea how long she had been unconscious, or for that matter, where she was. All she knew was it was getting dark, she had a large bleeding bump on her forehead, and she was soaked to the bone. With some effort, she carefully rolled her head to one side and surveyed her surroundings. Above her was a metal pipe set in cement that served as a handrail for the steps. Grabbing it for balance, she raised her shoulders slightly for a better look.

Several metal benches dotted a wide grassy area; between them was some sort of metal telescope and beyond that a stone wall. Behind her were the granite steps that led up to the parking lot. Her car was right where she left it. *That's right; I'm at a scenic overlook.* Her mind was beginning to focus. *I'm at a scenic overlook in the Smoky Mountains of North Carolina.* Struggling to orient herself, she saw the events that led her to this spot flashing behind her eyes in gut-twisting little vignettes. It took only seconds before full memory came flooding back.

Jane squeezed her eyes tightly shut trying to blot out the advancing pictures, but it did no good. The recall was bright and clear. There was a shot of her standing in her editor's office at the newspaper the day she got laid off. Another vivid snippet showed her live-in boyfriend telling her, yet again, how much better off she'd be if she just let him run her life. Several other images showed her sitting zombie-like, nurturing the nagging feeling that she was missing the point of life and the key was just beyond her reach. Then, as an added bonus, there were several bits and pieces of her praying to a so-far silent God for direction and clarity. Those particular scraps shot ripples of anger and despair through her in waves.

Jane grimaced at the recollections. *Well, I'm alive and I know who I am. My luck, I can't even manage a small case of amnesia.* Jane slowly rolled herself into a sitting position to take stock of her injuries. Her inquiring hands found a throbbing forehead and a couple of matching scrapes that her shins suffered when they slid over step number six. She was a bit dizzy so she sat motionless, still clinging to the metal rail, and waited for the sensations to pass. The bump on her forehead was the size of a ping pong ball but the cut wasn't deep. The rain mixing with what little blood there was gave the illusion of a much more grave injury. Jane wiped at her face with the hem of her blouse. Having checked out the physical, she began taking stock of her mental condition.

Discontent had been Jane's companion for a long time now, ever since her life had digressed into one long series of dramas and disappointments. This wasn't the way she planned it would go. Plowing through her days like a vehicle that was missing its steering wheel or a boat without a rudder, she was never quite in control. For all her best-laid plans, life seemed determined to waft along on whatever fickle breeze of chance blew her way. She had lost her connection, lost the ability to grasp the meaning of life and her purpose in it—that she was here for a reason.

Nothing was turning out the way she wanted it to, the way she used to see it in her dreams, and she was angry. Angry with her journalism degree: for all the long years of education, she still hadn't written anything that mattered. She was livid with her boyfriend for not being the man she needed him to be. She was outraged that all she thought her life could be was evaporating in front of her eyes like so much mist. Most of all, at the top of her list, she was furious with God.

Jane cradled her aching head in her hands and sighed, trying to push her thoughts aside for just another moment. What she wouldn't give for a good night's sleep—seven or eight uninterrupted hours, devoid of all the tossing and turning that takes place when the problems of the waking hours slop over into the night. She hardly dreamed anymore, not the good kind of dreams anyway. Now her hours of darkness were filled with second guesses and anxious questions. It was as if she had been dropped into a black hole with no exit, and lost in this void was the ability to navigate the road her life had taken—heck, she couldn't even find the path anymore. She'd developed a blind spot or taken a wrong turn somewhere, gotten off course, and she was suffering the avalanche of consequences of some foolish misstep.

Sitting on the steps, rain dripping from her long dark hair, Jane was fully back now, in body and of sound mind. Fully back and remembering the moments before her little accident. She had pulled into the tourist site just down the road from the cabin she was staying in to have a look. She'd passed it several times and each time she passed, she'd promised herself to stop. Curiosity had gotten the better of her today and it was time to make good on her promise. It would be a quick stop, just a minute to take a peek. The groceries, including her favorite brand of ice cream, were stowed in the back of her SUV and wouldn't allow her the luxury of a long idle. It wouldn't do for her double-brownie chocolate fudge to melt. She'd been looking forward to finding tonight's brand of comfort at the end of a spoon.

Jane raised her head and looked out on the vista before her. She didn't have a clue how long she'd been here, but the light was fading and fog crawled along the floor of the valley. The mountains had become little islands of muted color shrouded in a sea of gray. It seemed like only moments ago the sky had been a clear Carolina blue and the mountains stretched out before her like some magnificent rumpled quilt. Autumn had arrived and painted the landscape in a perfect mix of color. Amber, magenta, russet, greens, and yellows were so perfectly blended that if the scene were a painting, one would swear the artist took liberty with his rendering. Each mountain rose and fell in such a way there was no doubt that some divine hand had surely touched and molded each one. Seeing it reminded Jane that God not only existed but was very much present...and that's when the fight began.

Seeing all that beauty had thrown Jane into a mixture of awe and the sacred feeling you get when you know something is holy. It reminded her of her unanswered prayers and the silence that picked at the seams of her faith. She ranted, unleashing all the months of frustration. There had been pleading, even threatening, but in the end she was met with the same thundering stillness as before, as if she weren't significant enough or worthy of help. Adding insult to injury, the skies had opened and the rain pelted down on her. Turning to flee, the toe of her shoe slipped off the edge of the slick steps and she'd fallen. Now here she sat, wet and bloodied, on her own again to figure things out.

Jane took a deep breath. The dizziness had all but passed and she needed to get back to the cabin and take care of herself. Slowly she rose and tested her legs. *Well, looks like I'm going to live. My life is a shambles, I've lost my job, and my live-in boyfriend isn't even close to committing. I have very little money, I've lost my dreams, and today I had a fight with God, so I won't count on any help from anywhere. I'm on my own. Maybe I should become an atheist. Maybe it wouldn't be so bad living without heaven or angels or the belief that my life may have some meaning. I should go back to Atlanta and find a chapter of Atheists Anonymous and just soldier on.*

Jane pressed her hand to her head, trying to staunch the oozing blood. She spoke out loud to the sky. "I'm still mad at You, God, if You're even listening and I doubt You are. I am going to stop believing. Maybe mankind is nothing more than some accidental by-product of some primordial ooze. So, if You won't show me the way, I'll find my own way."

"I'll help you find your way," a small voice announced off to her left.

Jane turned her throbbing head, looking for the owner of the voice. Twisting around, she looked behind her; the only vehicle in the parking lot was hers. She peered into the growing darkness beyond the street lamp searching for a silhouette. The only thing she saw was a spider-web attached to the underside of the handrail.

"What?"

"I said, I can help you find the way." The disembodied voice came again. It sounded like a little old lady, small, but one that time hadn't robbed of her strength.

Jane screwed herself around again, trying to get an audio fix on the direction of the voice.

"Where are you?" she asked.

"Under here. I watched you fall; are you okay? I must say, wisdom should tell you not to run on wet stones. They grow moss, you know, and that can be very slippery when it's wet."

Jane's eyes darted back and forth as she made casual conversation. "Yeah, well, I don't feel very wise at the moment." She wondered if her vision had been affected by the blow to her head. "I still don't see you; could you show yourself?"

"Right here," the voice continued. "You looked right at me when you woke up. I'm here, below the handrail in my silk." Jane sat down on the step once again to get a better look at the rail.

Silk...who would wear silk in the rain? At that moment her eye caught the spider-web again. Her mind moved in staccato deliberations...Silk...spider-web...spider-silk. Jane slid her body closer to the handrail and squinted in concentration. There, resting in the center, was a small brown spider.

"There, that's better. I believe you can see me quite clearly now." The voice seemed to originate from the center of the web where the spider sat.

"Oh no...no, no, no, no, NOOO," Jane gasped, and in spite of her head, scrambled up the remaining steps to the parking lot. "Wrong, wrong, wrong, something is very wrong here." Thrusting her hand in her pocket she fumbled for her keys. She beeped her car open and threw herself in the driver's seat. "I have to get home; everything will be okay if I can get home. Oh my God, I'm hearing things. I thought I heard that spider speak to me. What's worse, I was talking back. I must have a head injury; the fall must have been harder than I thought. Doctor—maybe I need a doctor. That's exactly what I need; I'll go to the emergency room."

Jane's car spit gravel as she backed up and sped out of the parking lot. "Not too fast," she reminded herself. "Don't drive too fast; these county roads are narrow and wet. Remember you have a head injury."

What if I pass out before I get to the hospital? Her mind raced ahead even as she fought to keep her speed slow. Sitting forward in the seat she grasped the wheel with shaking hands. She had made it a point to locate all the important services when she arrived in town and knew the hospital was only about ten minutes away. "Drive slowly and concentrate on the road, you'll get there just fine," she coached herself as she maneuvered the SUV along the shiny black pavement.

The drive seemed like it took forever, but she managed to arrive without further incident. She parked the car and found the emergency room entrance without any trouble. She must have been a sight because the receptionist on duty pressed several buttons and immediately two nurses appeared out of nowhere.

She told the doctor she slipped on some slimy stones and banged her head—carefully omitting her conversation with a spider. She simply explained she wanted to be checked out in case there was some internal injury. There wasn't. The doctor told her even though she had a nasty bump, more than likely she had caught herself soon enough to prevent any real damage. He didn't see much evidence of a concussion, though there might be a slight one. Just in case, she wasn't to go to sleep for several hours and if, during that time, she experienced no nausea or dizziness, she would be fine. If she did, or if the pain got any worse, she was to come back.

He doesn't need to worry about me sleeping. There was no way she could close her eyes until she could find some plausible explanation for a talking spider. This wasn't one of those things one can shrug away and then toddle off to bed for a good night's sleep. She wouldn't be coming back to the hospital either, if she could help it. Her story had managed to escape any real scrutiny the first time, but she might not be so lucky the next time around. She could imagine the conversation.

"Why do you feel there must be something wrong?" the doctor would ask.

"Well, I heard this spider speaking to me right after I fell," Jane would answer.

"A spider you say. And this spider spoke to you?" the doctor would go on.

"Well, yes, that's why I'm worried," Jane would explain.

"Uh-huh. Nurse, would you draw Ms. Morgan's blood and have it tested for drugs and alcohol please, and…transfer her to the 'quiet room'." She would end up in some loony bin or rehabilitation center somewhere deep in the woods and never be heard from again. They would fit her for a white coat and she wouldn't have to worry another moment about the purpose or meaning of life. Someone else would be making all her decisions for her. When friends and family found out about her little accident, they would just shake their heads and say, "I always knew there was something not quite right about her." Jane rubbed her hands over her face. Except for the white jacket it would be kind of like her life now. Someone else always seemed to have their hand on the control buttons.

The rest of her visit went smoothly and two hours, several x-rays and a bandage later, Jane was home, dry and sitting on the sofa. The opening monologue of a late-night talk show was in full swing, but she wasn't paying attention to the television. She didn't even miss the ice cream that had melted hours ago in the back seat of her car. There would be no artificial comfort tonight. Lost deep in thought, Jane was searching her mental bank for any plausible explanation for what she had seen and heard. Nothing came to mind.

Along about 4 a.m. Jane's thoughts turned from fear to curiosity. How could this have happened? How was she able to hear a spider speak? Did it really speak, or was it her imagination or some hallucinatory hangover from being unconscious? At 5:50 a.m. Jane decided she had to find some answers rather than wonder for the rest of her life. At 7:15, as the sun was beginning to rise, Jane was dressed and ready to revisit the scenic overlook. She wanted to be sure she was sane. She could live with it then. The whole incident would become one of those stories you told when the conversation got around to seeing ghosts or making contact with the other side. A strange but true offering one could relate, and then laugh about.

Jane ate one of the blueberry muffins she had purchased the day before. She'd experienced no nausea and the pain had faded to no more than a sore spot on her forehead. She was physically okay, but her sanity was definitely in question. Maybe it was a result of the internal conversation she had right before the fall. Giving up on any help from God was a shattering event. Realizing there was nothing here to guide her in life felt like the bottom of the barrel she had dropped into months ago. *At least there is a bottom,* Jane mused as she drove down the driveway to the main road: *Beats the heck out of this constant free-fall through nothing.* Even if there was no light at the end of the tunnel, at least she had found the tunnel's end.

The SUV seemed to find its way back to the overlook on its own. Jane had been so deep in thought she couldn't remember driving; her mind was focused on finding an explanation. She wondered if maybe that's why you saw people in institutions talking to trees or rocks. Maybe they'd found the end of the tunnel too and the realization was so profound they snapped. For the second time in twenty-four hours, Jane locked her purse in the car and made her way to the stone steps. She'd make this quick. She would go down to the spider-web, say hi, get no reply, and get out of there. Then she could put the entire episode down as a freak accident.

As Jane hit step number one she mused about the kind of story she might write about this experience. *There may be a silver lining in this particular cloud. I could sell the article to some obscure magazine like* Too Far Out There to be Believable *or* Nutcase Monthly. *At least I could say I'd been published.* At step number two Jane located the spider's web at the handrail's intersection of the vertical and horizontal pipes. Before she could get comfortable or even focus, she heard the same tiny voice that had plagued her thoughts all night.

"Welcome back. I knew you would come."

TWO

...perhaps taking leave of your senses is the only way you will ever come to them

Jane's whole body went rigid. She couldn't breathe or think, nor could she look away from the web. At that moment, no force on Earth could have moved her; she was riveted. Shock robbed her of her voice, and several silent seconds passed before the spider spoke again.

"Ah...I see you're shaken by my greeting, Jane. You needn't be. It's really not all that extraordinary to talk to a spider, or any other living creature, for that matter. This is the way it's supposed to be, the oneness of all things, the way it was in the beginning."

Jane sputtered, trying to find her voice. "I'm insane...it's true; I hit my head and scrambled my brains and now I'm completely bonkers."

"No dear, you're not insane," the spider said with a little laugh. "But it did take that fall to slow you down enough to bring you to this moment. Perfect isn't it, how all things conspire for our highest good?"

Jane felt a twinge of agitation. "I would hardly call bashing your head against a rock perfect."

"I know, dear, nothing has seemed perfect for a long time, has it?" The spider folded her two front legs like you'd imagine your sympathetic grandmother would clasp her hands together right before she offered you a cookie.

Jane put her hands up and fingered the bandage on her forehead. She might have to make a trip back to the hospital after all. The whole white-coat scenario was looming larger by the moment. For the time being, as long as she was there, she might as well play along with her hallucination. "No, it hasn't been perfect, not even close. How did you know?"

"Oh, I know a great many things about you, dear, because I am *your* spider."

It was a long moment before Jane spoke again. She knew she was being drawn into a conversation by a figment of her imagination, but she was curious. "My spider?" she said.

"Yes, every human has a spider and I'm yours."

"Okay, you're going to have to explain this to me."

The tiny spider sighed, "Okay…hmmm, where to begin?"

"Oh, just go for it," Jane replied sarcastically.

"Surely," the spider answered as she sat back in the web and crossed six of her legs. "Well, the best place to begin is the beginning." The little brown spider cleared her throat and began. "These mountains are the oldest in the world. They are even older than the Azores. Did you know that, Jane?"

"No, I didn't," Jane said, leaning in a bit. Despite herself, she was growing more and more interested in the little spider's story.

"Well, it's true. It is also true that the oldest mountain in the world is right here in North Carolina. It's called Grandfather Mountain. Very appropriate, don't you think? Your geologists have dated the Grandfather to be more than a billion years old. It was the first mountain created and remains the father of all the mountains existing today. This is a known fact. What isn't known and rarely told is that hidden on one side of Grandfather Mountain is a tiny opening to a cave that is the home of Grandmother Spider…the very first spider.

"She is the keeper of secrets and the first scribe. It is she who records the history of the world. All that has ever happened is woven in the silk of her tremendous web. Her children, the writing spiders, have been charged with the same purpose she chose for our kind long ago. Each of us is destined to write history in our webs. Indeed, we are the only creatures on Earth, save humans, that can do so." The little spider stopped for a moment and looked straight into Jane's eyes. "So you see, I am a grandmother spider too and I am very proud of my lineage. Some of us write about world events, some record the weather, while others write the history of humans. It is my charge to write your history."

Jane's mouth dropped open. "My history!" she exclaimed. "What could be so important about me that you would want to record my history?"

"Each being that lives has importance, Jane; none is greater or smaller than the next. Each has a place in the events of the world and a reason for being here. You see, all of us share this wonderful Earth, and our lives naturally intersect. We live in relationship with each other, crossing paths and causing change to happen, for better or for worse. It is for this reason each person in the world has a writing spider whose job it is to record those changes. The spider marks their coming in and their leaving and all that happens in between; their lives, their loves, the children, the sorrows, the trials and triumphs… every bit of it.

"We keep the records of life on Earth. It is said that within everyone lies a book, a great autobiography of a life lived. But not everyone, fool or wise man, puts pen to paper leaving his history behind for others to read. Yet each life contains undeniable meaning and leaves its mark on the world, so each is recorded…because *each* makes a difference.

"So it has been from the beginning; all humans have been gifted with their very own writing spider who witnesses the movement of their days and seals their remarkable happenings with their webs. Because I am your spider, Jane, each strand of my web is a choice you made or a path you trod, up to this very day. Come closer and have a look."

Jane slid closer to the handrail and stared intently at the web. It was larger than she had first perceived. Parts of the web had a beautiful and intricate pattern, woven in perfectly symmetrical designs. Each strand led to another and still another until a magnificent pattern emerged. There were other threads, too—strands that crossed and doubled back again and thin strings of silk that didn't connect to anything, simply floating, waving gently in the breeze. Then there were spaces and holes where it seemed something should be, but remained empty.

Jane was fascinated with the patterns and the faults of the web. She spoke without looking away, "This is the story of my life, right here in this web?"

"Yes, dear, I chose to record your life and keep it safe. Can you see it written in my language? Look closely. Some parts are perfect, while others are full of doubt and U-turns where something was ventured and not completed. Sometimes you would go back and start again, and other times you gave up. Those are the strands that are not attached, floating and incomplete. These disconnected threads are choices and commitments you made and never carried through. They tell of the times you doubted yourself and lacked the courage to act. The strands that do connect tell of promises kept and lessons completed. Those create the most beautiful patterns.

"All in all, there is a grace to it, an elegant beauty. You're really doing rather well. Every day I write a bit more. See here?" Grandmother Spider pointed to a large space. "This is where we are today, and this hole is waiting for me to weave together how you choose to move next."

Jane sat back. "That's the million-dollar question, isn't it? How I choose to move next. That's why I'm here, why I left Atlanta for a month, to figure all that out."

"I know, Jane," Grandmother replied tenderly.

"How do you know? For that matter, how do you know what to record? You live here under this handrail and I've lived so many different places, in Atlanta, at college, back at home. Who tells you what to write?"

"Oh, that's easy, dear. We all know what we all know, Jane." Grandmother Spider noticed the puzzled look on Jane's face and went on, "Humans think they are individuals, disconnected from each other, separate from the rest of creation. But we are actually all part of each other, made of the same material and by the same hand. We are all part of the same one thing...the only thing there is. If you can understand this you will come to understand how we all know what we all know."

Jane paused for a moment, trying to grasp the meaning of what seemed to be a riddle. "Are you saying our minds belong to some sort of great communal mind?"

"In a sense, yes, they all do." Reading Jane's confusion, Grandmother continued, "It's like the radio you listen to. There are different stations on different frequencies. It's all a matter of what you're tuned to. Humans tend to stay on one frequency and tune everything else out. It's much easier for animals and plants, my dear. We've stayed more closely connected to the Earth by choice and also by necessity. This is the reason we are more finely tuned to her frequencies. We live on instinct and have inherited purpose, something you folks don't really have. While it's true you have the instinct to survive and you are programmed for the finer points, you rarely tune into anything but your immediate needs.

"Our survival depends on us hearing each other and recognizing the signs and signals. In my case, I am always alert for a hungry bird looking for lunch or a storm full of wind. I can gather the information I need from listening to the trees or watching my animal brothers and sisters. Sometimes I just break down and ask."

"You mean you can speak to each other—other animals—like a common language?" Jane stared in disbelief.

"Certainly, Jane, how do you think I am talking to you?"

"Okay, we're going too far here. I don't know whether I can buy the whole communal mind and common language concept."

"Well, if you aren't going to try to understand, Jane, you will never get the answers you seek. Your spirit will never heal," Grandmother Spider admonished her. "You asked God for help. Now are you willing to entertain the answers or not?"

Although Jane couldn't see the features of the diminutive face clearly, she knew Grandmother Spider was scowling at her.

"Sorry," Jane said, "I'm just put out with God right now. I'm not even sure He exists."

"Yes, I know you are, honey, but if you're patient and open to the answers, you will learn all you need to know and then some. And by the way, God not only exists, He is very present."

"Well, you couldn't prove it by me," Jane retorted. "He hasn't been very present in my life the past couple of years. Believe me, I've been looking. If He is so present, why isn't He talking to me?"

"It's not so much about *God* answering your prayers and fulfilling your wishes, Jane, it's about *you* fulfilling them. You have been gifted with everything you could ever need or want to succeed at what you choose. The power to create the life you wish is yours. So the answer to your question is both your blessing and your curse. It lies in the gift of free will. You get to choose whatever you wish to see, hear and experience. If you choose to believe in the oneness of everything, you can tune into everything that is. That's where God lives and speaks. If you choose to believe such oneness does not exist, then for you, it will not. *It is done unto you as you believe.*"

"I don't know what to believe anymore. My life is such a mess. Every choice I make seems to be worse than the one before. I'm to the point where I am afraid to make a choice. It seems like everything I touch destroys itself in the end."

"When you lose your way, as you have now, you become deaf and blind to all the opportunity lying before you. The only control you have left is over destruction. If you cannot see forward, then you stare backwards into what has already passed away. If you can't create, then you can only destroy. It's one or the other, like night and day. There is no in between, no standing still.

"Sometimes a thing must be destroyed to make way for a new, more wonderful thing. You can't build a new home where an old shack stands without first tearing down the shack. But the same tools you use to tear down, you can use to build up. Wouldn't you love to have the tools to control the way your life goes? Wouldn't you love to strip away all the drama and pain that comes with destruction and create situations and relationships you really love?"

"Well, yes, who wouldn't?" mused Jane. "But God didn't leave any blueprint on how to build a great life. You aren't born with a handbook that tells you how life works or what choices to make. There aren't any burning bushes or red flags that pop up to let you know this job isn't for you or this person isn't your soul mate. It's all just whim or chance. You simply meet whatever life throws at you the best you can and take your lumps. Like the old saying goes, you play the hand you're dealt."

"I'm sure that's how it all appears to you, Jane, but that's not exactly true. Life doesn't have to be haphazard; you don't have to take everything that comes your way, good or bad, and feel it's meant to be. Destiny isn't determined by a flip of the coin or some cruel chess game the Fates play for their own amusement.

"As far as playing the hand you're dealt, you're playing with the wrong deck. You're using the wild cards thrown at you by life. These are discards from the people and situations you find yourself faced with; you don't have to pick all of them up. The real canasta was dealt at your birth, and how you play it, and when, is what determines the quality of the life you live."

Jane pondered Grandmother's words. "You may be right, but once you're standing in a pile of rubble, you're afraid to play another card, terrified you're headed for another disaster."

"Yes, I know it seems that way now, yet it wasn't always so. Look here at this spot in my web. See here? This pattern is the day you had your first ballet recital. I believe you were seven. You were so afraid to go on stage, scared you would forget the steps or lose your timing, and yet you still went on. You overcame your fear and your doubts. You refused to be defeated by them and you danced. Look at how the threads sparkle. They dance in the light, just as you did that day, and the joy of that moment still shines today.

"And here, look at this thread. This is the day you changed. You allowed fear into your life. Somehow what you felt about yourself and what was possible for you didn't matter anymore. Instead, you worried how others felt about you, what they saw when they looked at you. In that instant you gave up the power you once had to choose your own path. It was a sad day for me when I recorded this piece." Grandmother dabbed at her eyes with one little leg while another patted the forlorn string.

"Over here, this dangling strand is unattached because you quit. Remember your dream of becoming the editor of your college newspaper? You *really* wanted that job, Jane; you were passionate about it and more than qualified for it. But when you found out how many others were applying, you doubted your talent. You didn't even fill out the application. You weren't rejected for the position, you simply quit. You defeated yourself. Why? Out of fear…Where was the spirit of the brave little ballerina that day?"

"I don't know," Jane whispered, closing her eyes to the web. "I don't know who I am anymore, or why I'm even here."

"I know you don't, my dear, but that's why you're here now, speaking to me. You say God isn't present for you and that He doesn't speak to you anymore, but how did this meeting come to be? You asked for it, you prayed for it, and now you will be graced with the answers. You will be shown what your kind has forgotten. You will understand the nature of life and what guides God has placed on Earth, not only for you, but for everyone who chooses to see them."

"What do you mean 'I'll be shown'?" Jane jerked her head up, her eyes widening. "Is there more?"

"Oh yes, Jane, much more. The next one you speak with will be your permanent escort for the rest of your journey. There will be others too, waiting to tell you their stories and eager to teach their lessons. This is why you're here, to discover your blueprint for living life on Earth. I know it doesn't feel like it, Jane, but you've been

19

guided and nudged, urged to be in this place in time. Still, in the end, you are the one who chose it. You're never as alone as you believe you are, Jane...*never*. You're about to discover God in more places than just prayer.

"The best part for me is I will be the one to write it. It's perfect, Jane, a writing spider for a writer. When this web is finished, it will be the story of your life and the purpose and the meaning of mine. The pattern, I hope, will be magnificent and filled with the reason for your presence on Earth. Try to see the beauty and the gift that's your life, Jane, and you may find the wealth of wisdom you long for.

"Only a lucky few have even glimpsed into their lives in such a way. But remember this, I am merely the scribe who records what is; it is you who chooses the direction your story will take. You create the plot by the choices you make and the actions you take...Choose wisely, Jane." With that, the tiny scribe turned her back to Jane and went to work.

Feeling her visit drawing to a close, she called out to Grandmother, "Wait, why can't you be my escort? For that matter, why can't you just tell me what I need to know, the rules of the game? I'm a quick study."

"Oh, my dear, I have chapters and chapters to write; besides, if I told you all you will come to know you will never experience your own wisdom or know your own worth. I can't tell you, Jane; for your answers to be true, they must come from within. As for being your escort, I am much too small and fragile to be of any great help. Still, I will know every step you take and I will be with you in spirit."

"Yes...okay...well, goodbye Grandmother, and thank you. Maybe taking leave of my senses won't be such a bad thing after all."

Grandmother turned and looked at Jane with a smile. "Maybe taking leave of your senses is the only way you will ever come to them." Grandmother winked at Jane as she turned back to her web once more and began humming quietly to herself.

Reluctantly, Jane climbed back up the steps to the parking lot. Part of her was saddened by the end of today's meeting, while the other part anticipated the next chapter of her strange odyssey. *Maybe I, too, will have chapters and chapters to write when this is over.* She grinned to herself. *That is, if they allow me a pen in the loony bin.*

THREE

...the dominion we think we hold is an illusion...in the grand scheme of things, we are just one part of the mystery

Jane drove slowly back to the cabin. She had come to it by way of a favor. Her best friend's parents bought it years ago as a weekend getaway. With their children grown and retirement looming, they were going to sell the place along with its five acres and buy something a bit more suited to their needs. The down-swing in the housing market made it clear the house would be empty for a while, and they had offered Jane the opportunity to use it for a month after she got laid off. Jane needed this time away to sort out the mess her life had become, and she pinned a lot of hope on the idea that this solitude could bring her some sort of insight and clarity. She needed to reevaluate everything—life, love, career, her faith—and take a new course of action. In her heart she secretly feared she was on a fool's errand. If she couldn't get her life together in Atlanta, what made her think she could magically get it together here? A change of location just changes the scenery, not the person. You could run, but you sure couldn't hide.

Jane's stomach rumbled, drawing her attention back to the present. Her head was as full as her stomach was empty. What a difference twelve hours could make. Even though her first encounter with Grandmother left her shocked and doubting her own sanity, little by little, it became comfortable. There was a familiarity to it and, she had to admit, it made her feel special. She had a secret she would jealously guard and, even though she still doubted her sanity, a small sliver of hope was taking root. That was more than she'd had in a long while.

Back in Atlanta she'd felt so desperate she'd even tried a prayer-line, one of those people at the end of a telephone that God found good enough and spiritual enough to listen to, intermediaries for those who couldn't find their way to God themselves. Jane never knew where she was on their list, but it must have been pretty far down because nothing changed. No light broke over the horizon. Perhaps she kept getting moved down in status as others with more pressing problems sought the group's service. After all, she was relatively young and very healthy, nothing as urgent as dying from some terrible disease, war or mass starvation. She was simply a woman who couldn't seem to keep her life together. The prayer circle may have judged her problems too small, just another whiney broad who could wait.

But that was then and not today. Today Jane knew two things for sure: One, she would never again look at the world in quite the same way. The conversation had opened her to the knowledge that human beings were not the absolute masters of the planet. *The dominion we think we hold is an illusion. In the grand scheme of things, we are just one part of the mystery.* The second thing she knew for sure: She would never kill another spider as long as she lived.

Jane drove the little country road recalling Grandmother's words: *"The next one you speak with will be the permanent escort for the rest of your journey."* She wondered who or what the *next one* would be.

Her feelings were a mixture of anticipation and apprehension. Would he or she be at the cabin waiting for her or would she have to wait a while? The Grandmother also told Jane that a tiny spider was much too fragile to be of any great help. Did that mean her escort would be big and burly like a bear or a mountain lion? Meeting a tiny spider was one thing, but settling your nerves around a bear would be quite another. This was uncharted territory so she didn't know what to expect. Heck, in the woods of these mountains, it could be an elf or a fairy. Jane drew a mental picture in her mind of her own personal Tinkerbell, wings and all.

Wings, Jane thought, *wings...wouldn't it be great if it were an angel.* Her imagination conjured angels with lovely iridescent wings, glowing and beautiful to behold. An angel would certainly prove that God still cared about her, and Grandmother Spider had mentioned her spirit needed healing. Yes, an angel would be all the proof she would ever need; it had to be an angel. Anticipation forced Jane's foot to press harder on the gas pedal.

She wondered if her angel would teach her at the cabin or bear her up on his wings and fly her places she had never been. What would his voice sound like? Which angel would it be—Metatron, the king of angels, regal and majestic, or the mighty warrior Michael, come to do battle for her sore little soul? Jane's stomach rumbled. *Whoever it is, I hope he'll wait until I have something to eat.*

Jane made the turn into her driveway and noticed a cardinal sitting on an oak branch hanging over the lane. She waved to the bird without thinking. It burst into song as she passed. *Oh my God,* she thought, *they do recognize us. Maybe they've just been waiting, all this time—eons—for us to recognize them.*

As she pulled up to the cabin, her eyes searched the yard and the woods, but she saw no divine glow. She sat in the car for a moment surveying the area. The property itself was a bit overgrown and wild. Nature was steadily stealing back what was hers to begin with. The hand-hewn logs begged for a fresh coat of stain, and the furniture inside was of the second-hand childproof vintage, but with the right touches the place could be one of those charming cottages one saw in magazines. At the moment, all Jane cared about was it had a television, a place to plug in her computer, a bed, and something to cook on. She was out of the city and for the first time in a long time she felt like she could breathe—for a month at least. Still, she felt at home here, spared from the constant confrontation with the wreckage that was her life in Atlanta.

When nothing showed itself outside, Jane finally got out of the SUV and walked to the front door. She turned her body in complete circles, looking around as she went. Nothing…No heavenly hosts appeared, no divine music played…nothing but birds singing and leaves rustling.

Jane let herself into the house half-expecting to find her angel sitting on the couch waiting. Peering down the hall, she made her way into the kitchen; the cabin was empty and quiet. Maybe her escort knew she needed to eat and rest before beginning this leg of her journey.

Jane took bread, lunch meat and cheese from the refrigerator and set about making her lunch. *Guess I'll just have to wait till he shows himself. If he'd hurry I'd invite him to eat with me.* It struck her then that angels didn't have to eat, sleep or do any of the things humans did. As divine beings they had none of the needs a human body did. *How sad,* she thought, *never knowing what roast beef and cheddar cheese tastes like, or the feeling of clean sheets on your bed. How incredibly blessed we humans are to have the abilities of our five senses. We take so much for granted.* Jane wondered if she ever expressed any gratitude for the tastes and smells and feelings she experienced. *What a gift.*

She placed her sandwich on a plate, grabbed a glass of milk and headed out the back door as she mentally cataloged dozens of her favorite feelings, tastes and smells. *What would life be without them?* Jane took a deep breath. *This smell is definitely on my list of favorites: fresh air and pine needles.*

The back porch was screened. The furniture was a mish-mash of yard-sale bargains, and she suspected this wide space had served as somewhere young children could enjoy the fresh air and vent their energy on rainy days. She placed her lunch on an ancient picnic table that bore the scars of a pen knife and sat down to eat. She was chewing her first bite when she heard a voice say, "Hey!"

Jane almost choked trying to swallow fast enough to answer. Out of the corner of her eye she caught a slight movement by the screen door. What her eyes beheld was no heavenly host. Standing where her angel should have been was one of the scruffiest, dirtiest dogs imaginable.

Her sandwich dropped to the plate. "It's you, isn't it?" she said with a trace of disappointment in her voice. "My escort?"

"Geez, I'm not that bad," the dog answered. "I know I haven't had a bath lately, but I've been on my own for a while."

Jane was utterly speechless as she pushed open the screen door. The dog brushed past her at mid-thigh and sat down near the table. An ironic smile spread across Jane's face. Here she had been dreaming of some divine and angelic visitation and instead what she got was a mutt. She would remind herself in the future to give up on her expectations and allow things to unfold as they would.

Neither spoke as they took measure of each other. Bath or no bath, the dog was by no means a purebred anything—maybe a cross between a golden retriever and a collie or a chow or a...something.

His coat was thick, longish and a light shade of gold all over, but his fur was matted in spots, crusted with red dirt and something brown and sticky. One ear bore a healed rip from an old injury by who knows what, and when his mouth was closed, his top right canine tooth stuck out over his bottom lip.

"Disappointed?" he said.

Jane cleared her throat. "No, not really," she answered, trying to be casual and polite. "I just thought you would…I just imagined you…ah, a bit cleaner and maybe a bit more divine."

"Ah, the *Angel* wish," Dog said.

Jane blushed and looked down at her feet; there was no use denying it. An awkward moment passed as Jane struggled to change the subject.

"So I take it you don't have a home? You're a stray?" Jane asked, relieved to move on from the topic of angels.

"Yup, I'm a stray; I had a home once, but not now."

"Well, do you have a name?"

"I've had several," the dog replied. "I've been called Rex, Goldie, Bandit, and a few others I won't mention in polite company. Those more colorful names were temporary and usually came after I'd been caught rifling through someone's trash can."

Jane stared at the dog. He wasn't as unattractive as she first thought; with a good bath, there were possibilities. She wondered how attractive she would be if she were homeless.

"How did you get the job of my escort?"

"Escort is Grandmother Spider's description. I prefer the term *guide*—and to answer your question, the call went out on the wind. I wasn't exactly busy so I volunteered."

"Call…what call? Or rather *who* called?" Jane was curious and still trying to digest the idea of this universal mind.

"You did, Jane, don't you remember? You were crying out for answers." The dog saw the blank look on Jane's face as she struggled to make sense of his answer so he continued. "When you wish for something or seek something, your thoughts naturally dwell on that wish. Thoughts are a form of energy that radiate out much the same way a radio station is able to send music through the air. Grandmother mentioned this, remember? There are different frequencies for different energies. Trees have certain frequencies that are very different from, say, mice. If you're tuned in, you can pick these up. I picked up yours, so I came."

Jane nodded. She was getting the concept. "So you're my guide for the rest of this journey?"

"Yup, I am. I know what you were expecting," he said, "but your request was to find answers about life in the physical realm and that requires a physical guide. Angels spend their time on more, how shall I put this, more ethereal problems. Theirs is mostly an internal guidance, lots of inspiration and dream work, although they do intervene in the physical from time to time. If I read you right, you're a pretty smart cookie, but more of a *show-me* type. I am here to show you, clear the path for you."

Not dumb, by any means, Jane thought to herself as the dog lay down and crossed his two front paws. *Internal guidance*—her mind raced back to a few of her more memorable dreams and she wondered how many of those messages might have been angelic. *How many did I attribute to a late-night snack or an overactive imagination?*

The dog went on with his explanation. "Our kind has always served as guides for humans. Indigenous people have always had some form of canine as a guide—wolves, dogs, even coyotes—though the vast majority of humans never know it. People have such a talent for over-complicating their lives with the strangest stuff, they seldom have time to slow down and listen or just be. Always on the go. I've said it before and I'll say it again: most of the world's problems could be solved by a good nap or some time alone under the porch. Anyway…dog has always been man's best friend and as of today, I'm yours."

"When you explain it all that way, I am glad I have a dog as a guide. At home on the farm, we always owned dogs. All of them were considered to be members of the family and we loved them dearly." Jane felt like she was still rationalizing the angel preference.

"Most humans treat their dogs very well, but you just made a very interesting point. It's something I wish to point out with the understanding that your perspective of life could use some expansion."

"What's that?" Jane asked.

"You said you *owned* dogs. Have you ever considered you didn't own them so much as they *chose* to live with you?"

Jane blinked a couple of times. "Boy, you just get right to it, don't you?"

"That's what I'm here for. You see, the vast majority of your kind believe they have power over things they really don't control, and the real power you have, to change and create your lives and the world around you, you don't use or have no clue as to how it works. Humans have such a *thing* about ownership, not to mention control. You spend your entire lives racing about, trying to earn enough money to buy the things you believe you need to be happy, as if the one that owns the most will be the happiest. You don't really ever *own* anything, Jane, except the moment you are experiencing now.

"Your dogs chose to be with you because it was their purpose, because they loved you and because they invested lots of time and effort into training you to understand what they needed."

"Wow, I never quite looked at it that way, about control or my dogs. I guess my perspective does need some fine-tuning...And I thought this journey was going to be simple."

"It will be simple, Jane, if you let it."

"So, what about cats, what is the reason they stay with their human...friends?" Jane picked her words carefully. She saw a flicker of disgust run across the dog's face.

"I know why dogs stay. We're loyal and true; there's meaning to our being with humans. I think cats stay because you're tall enough to reach the kitchen cabinets and have the fingers and thumbs to open a tuna can."

Jane stifled a laugh; she wouldn't push the cat subject any further. "Oh my gosh, where are my manners? Speaking of food, are you hungry or thirsty? How about a bowl of water?"

"Now that you mention it, it's been a while since I've eaten, so both would be nice."

Jane moved to the kitchen and found two bowls. One she filled with water and in the other she placed the uneaten half of her sandwich. She sat in silence making a mental note to buy kibble while the dog slaked his thirst and gobbled down the sandwich. When he had finished she began the conversation again.

"I can see how changing my perspective about life and understanding its nature in a different way could bring a whole new level of richness to my life, but how will it solve my problems, like getting a job and making enough money to live?"

"Patience, Jane, give this some time. This is your experience and what you will take from it I can't predict. There is a difference between understanding and truly knowing. You can *understand* a concept but never really know how to anchor it in your life and use it to your benefit. When you *know,* then you are able to use it as a tool to build whatever you wish. You have brought yourself to this place and given yourself the time for this experience; it's up to you how you will use it."

"Will a month be enough time to know?"

"It will be if you let it. Time is a funny thing. Again, it's all about your perception. It can seem to drag in one moment, and in the next, everything is happening at once. You measure it with your watch and bind it by sunrises and sunsets, but truly, it can do as it wishes with you. Let time have its way with you, Jane—it's the only way you will know what it truly is."

Jane sighed in exasperation. "This feels like riddles to me. What if I don't figure this all out? How can I know then?"

"Give yourself a little credit, start believing in your ability. You'll see; it will all work out. You mentioned money—this is your biggest worry at the moment, isn't it?"

"It's right there at the top of the list. I can't think of anything more important right now," Jane replied.

"Then let's look at your money problem. First, how much money do you think you need? What's too little and how will you know when you have enough?"

Jane thought a moment. "Well, what I have in my bank account now feels like too little. I don't really know how much will be enough...I know it doesn't grow on trees."

"Maybe you don't know how much will be enough because you don't know what you want out of life? And as for growing on trees, you do realize it's just green paper, don't you?"

"Yes, of course I know it's green paper," Jane replied.

"Well then, in the truest sense, it really does grow on trees. Jane, think about it for a minute. You have given this green paper great power. It has that power because the human race agreed it has power and so it becomes the thing you seek the most."

Jane narrowed her eyes at the dog, not really seeing him. Her mind was too busy wrapping itself around the conversation. She had never actually analyzed money before and it did seem silly to place so much importance on mere paper, but she wasn't ready to give up on the idea so easily. After all, how could a dog understand money?

"Yes, but, if everyone agrees money is power, then it *becomes* powerful and if you don't have it, you don't have any power in this world. If I don't have it to pay my bills or buy food, then I become just like you, a homeless hungry stray." Jane regretted the homeless hungry remark the minute it came out of her mouth.

"In one way or another, we're all strays, Jane. Each of us has wandered from who we truly are, drifting from our dreams and separating from our souls. Some of us are lured away by the illusion of the greener pasture. Others seek all things bright and shiny, or drift down the path of least resistance. Then there are those hearts that suffer abandonment and are so scarred, they hide from life and guard their hearts from the light. Lost in the chaotic lives of our own making, we become orphans, disconnected from our true natures.

"But even strays can find their way home. Once lost does not have to become never found. The spirit is unbreakable and even though its voice may be silenced under the weight of a thousand bricks, the walls we construct will never hold against the knowledge that the soul is indestructible and evergreen. The first step in understanding the way home does not lie without, but within. The second step is merely choosing not to be homeless."

Jane looked into the dog's gentle brown eyes and found sympathy. He would be a kind and patient guide, but at the same time, he would speak the truth as he knew it. There would be no hedging or polite agreement with her muddy concepts of life; the guidance she would receive would be as crystal clear and unadulterated as nature herself. And that's just what she'd prayed for, clarity and direction.

She cleared her throat and went on, "What I mean to say is, money is a success marker. It defines how well you operate in the world."

"Exactly," the dog replied. "That's exactly how you measure your worth. It's a shame isn't it, that humans have created such a system. Money is a currency, Jane, but not the only one. Love, joy, comfort, peace, beauty, meaning, creativity, friendship, those are all currencies too. They mean something; without them what would life be? And yet you don't rate them as highly or think them to be as powerful as money. As a success marker, money is a pretty poor one. Would you call a man that enjoys the love of his wife and children unsuccessful?"

"Well…no," Jane stammered.

"Jane, you have free will; you can define your idea of what success is anytime you wish. You only need to be clear on what you want in your life and what you wish to experience as you're living. While I agree that humans need money as an exchange, it doesn't have to be a measure of your worth as a being. The richest people on Earth are those who have decided being wealthy is not related to money at all."

A silence grew between them and Jane knew the dog was giving her time to digest. She thought back to her reverie in the kitchen about angels and roast beef sandwiches. Just a little while ago, she had considered herself luckier than the heavenly hosts because of all the experiences that being in the physical world afforded her. And yet, in a short space of time, she had forgotten the joy of living and argued for a life of material objects. It was the sandwich not the money she had eaten, and the sandwich not the money that brought her pleasure. Her perspective on life and her priorities could certainly use some adjustment.

She needed to go back and figure out exactly what she wanted from her life. Maybe the dog was right: to know how much was enough and what meant the most was the gift and the real success marker. She was lost deep in thought when the dog spoke again.

"Perhaps we have gone too far in our first meeting. Think about it, Jane. I want you to think about the wealth of your life so far. It will be important as we go along for you to appreciate what you already have and what more you desire. You will not find your destination if you don't know where it is. For this journey to work, you must forget what you thought you knew about life, wake up and allow your mind to consider new ideas and concepts." Dog stood up and headed for the door. "I have to go. I just came by to introduce myself, tell you I was here, and we can start first thing in the morning."

"Go?" Jane asked quickly, "You're not staying here? I mean, I assumed you would be here all the time if you're my guide."

The dog looked surprised. "I hadn't really thought about it. I came to guide you; I never imagined you would want me to stay here in the meantime."

"Well, would you like to stay?" Jane held her breath. She had so many questions and thoughts to process, and it would be great to have him to talk it all out with. Besides, she was lonely. "If you wouldn't mind a bath, you could sleep in the house. These October nights are getting chilly."

The dog looked down at his paws and then up at Jane. His dark brown eyes held a hint of sadness. Jane wondered what memory he might be wrestling with. Suddenly he brightened a bit and asked, "Do you have a cat?"

"No, no cats," she answered.

"Then I would really like to stay and I don't mind a bath at all."

Jane was up on her feet in a second, chatting excitedly as she held the kitchen door open for Dog. "Great. As soon as we have you all cleaned up, we can take a ride to town and get you some dog food. Then tonight we'll build a fire and get to know each other a bit better. How does that sound?"

"Like heaven on Earth," Dog said as she led him down the hall to the bathroom.

FOUR

...it doesn't take a boulder

It took the better part of two hours to give Dog a bath and then clean the tub. Jane had never seen so much dirt come off one animal in her life. Lacking real dog products, she used her favorite raspberry-scented shampoo, and it had required two sudsings to get the job done. Jane jabbered as she worked.

"I remember when I was little my dad used to take me on fishing trips. Sometimes we would camp and fish for a couple of days. I loved being with him on those excursions, just me and him, alone in the woods, pitting our skills against the fish. But I also loved my bubble baths and complained loud and long about three or four days without a tub. Dad would laugh at me and tell me to go down to the lake and rinse off, but I couldn't stand the idea of being in there with all those fish. I thought it was yucky."

The dog snorted and shook his head. He seemed amused.

"What?" Jane asked.

Dog turned to look Jane in the face and said, "Yucky...That's exactly how fish feel when they see a human."

His revelation took her aback. She'd never wondered about other creatures' perceptions of the human form; before she could give it much thought the dog went on: "When you and your father were at the lake, did you ever skip stones or throw pebbles in the water?"

"Yeah, Dad taught me how to skip stones at that lake. In the evening I used to walk the shore alone and toss rocks. It was so peaceful there."

"Did you notice the ripples your rocks created when you threw them in?"

"Sure," Jane said as she worked his yellow fur into a lather once again.

"Good, then you will understand what I am about to tell you. I don't want to rush you into this, I know it's all so new, but there are some things you need to know at the beginning of our time together."

"No, you're not rushing me. I really want to know all of this. It is a bit new and I'm still adjusting to the whole talking-to-animals deal, but go ahead."

"Okay," Dog began. "I want you to remember how the ripples looked when the stone fell into the water. They start out small and tight and then grow larger, taking in more of the lake, pushing out from the spot the stone first went in. This is the way each creature affects life here on Earth.

"Imagine yourself the stone. Who you are and what you do affects the water and ripples out to include more and more of the lake. It is exactly the same in life. Who you are and what you do has an effect on those around you in ever-widening circles. The first tight ripple is self. What you choose and the actions you take regarding those choices influence the path and quality of your life. The ripple widens and includes those closest to you, like your mate and your family. The consequences of your actions, positive or negative, impact them also. The ripple grows wider yet and takes in your neighborhood or community and finally it grows to include the world.

"You think yourself small and of no consequence, but in truth, everything that lives makes its own ripple in the world. Grandmother Spider explained choice to you. She showed you in her web that you are where you are in life today because of the choices you made in your yesterdays. I want you to understand that those choices do not affect only you, but everyone."

"You're telling me that getting laid off from my job and leaving Atlanta affects everyone?" Jane challenged the dog. "I doubt my leaving the paper will cause much of a ripple; and leaving my boyfriend in Atlanta, well, he is probably happy I'm gone."

"Yes, that's exactly what I'm saying, Jane. You thought your writing meant nothing, but in truth, others read your words, and the way they thought, their attitude about life and the actions they took because of a new belief or idea you interjected may have affected the way they moved in the world. As for your boyfriend, whether he's glad you're gone or not, he will act differently and do different things now that he is alone. It doesn't take a boulder to create ripples—a very small pebble will do."

"Oh, I get it," Jane said, rinsing the suds from the yellow coat. "It's like that saying about the butterfly that flaps its wings in Africa causing a typhoon in Japan?"

"Yes, that's exactly the same idea."

"So what you're saying is as I go along figuring out my life and what I want, who I am and what I'm doing here, I shouldn't forget that what I choose will have an impact on others."

"Yes," the big dog replied.

"But I am not the only one making a choice. Everyone else is making them too. There are millions of ripples happening; don't they bump into each other?"

"Yes, Jane, they do and this is my point. The ripples bump into each other, they intersect all the time. Whether they meld together or crash into one another is the difference between harmony and disharmony...sometimes between peace and war."

Jane finished the final rinse, all the while thinking about ripples bumping into each other. The metaphor worked well. She could plainly see how each person moving in the world could create havoc or harmony, and attitude played a big part in whether their choices clashed or melted into one another. She even supposed money and greed had its part in the whole scenario. *I get it. He wants me to understand that while I am figuring out my life, I should take into consideration that my decisions will affect others. He wants me to be ready for what's to come.*

After the appropriate shaking and toweling, Dog was a different creature, brighter and more comfortable. He was a much different dog from the one she welcomed earlier in the day. Jane now found him handsome in a rugged sort of way. He jumped in the front seat of the SUV like a pro and stuck his nose out the window as they rode to town. Their conversation was easy, just two new friends getting to know one another.

Dog waited patiently in the car while Jane was in the grocery store. She had inquired about his preferences in kibble and bought the brand he liked best. On a whim, she asked the butcher if he had any bones. She managed to get a half dozen and hoped Dog would be pleased. She wanted to surprise him but she knew there was no hope of secrecy—he would smell them as soon as she was in the car.

"Bones?" he asked. "You got me bones?"

Jane laughed, and yet she thought she saw the same fleeting sadness cross his face that she had seen earlier when she asked him to stay.

"Sure," she said. "I like all my guests to enjoy their stay." Jane changed the subject. "What would you like me to call you? You never said which name you preferred, and Dog is a bit impersonal for me."

"Any of the names I mentioned before would be fine," he said with his nose stuck out the window again. It was said without conviction and a feigned lack of interest. What was behind his moments of sadness and his disinterest, she had no idea. She would ask him about it when they knew each other better.

"I don't think they suit you," Jane said. "Let's pick a new name. A new name for a new beginning...one you really like."

Dog turned from the window, his ear up. "Really? Well...I have always been partial to the name Max. I knew a dog named Max once. He was a good friend to me at a time when I needed it most."

"Okay, Max it is," Jane replied. "I like it too, and it suits you."

Jane and Max chatted back and forth through their dinner preparations. The meal was eaten mostly in silence and when Max finished, Jane offered him a bone. He lay on the floor and worked on his dessert while she put away the leftovers and washed the dishes. As she watched him, she wondered how long it had been since Max was full, warm and clean, all at the same time.

When all was done they moved to the living room, and true to her word, Jane built a fire. Max carried his bone with him and curled up on the braided rug. His eyes followed her movements, and when she was comfortably installed on the couch, the afghan tucked around her, he spoke. "No TV tonight?"

"No, I really don't watch much TV unless I am alone." Jane yawned. "Besides, I'm exhausted. I didn't sleep at all last night. I must be running on pure adrenaline. It's hard to believe it was just this morning I was chatting with a spider, and now here I am talking to a dog. I need to get my head around all of this."

"Yes, I can see how it would be a bit confusing," Max said.

"More like life-altering," Jane responded.

"You must have questions."

"Only about a million." Jane went on, "So many I don't even know where to start. I just need to be quiet and let it all sink in. I don't want to forget all the things Grandmother told me this afternoon. I don't want to forget anything. There's a lot to digest."

"Well, anything you want to talk about or ask, just let me know. That's why I'm here."

"Okay…do fish really think humans are yucky?" Jane asked with a smile.

Max returned the grin. "Yup…they're horrified." Both of them laughed, sympathizing with the fish.

"Seriously, there is one thing, Max, although in the midst of all of this I suppose it's minor, but I'm curious," Jane said as she adjusted the throw pillow under her head.

"What is it?"

"Earlier you said it was dog's purpose to be man's best friend."

"Yes, that's true."

"How did that come to be? Why was the dog chosen to be man's best friend—why not a bird or a cat?"

"Dogs weren't chosen, dogs chose to be man's best friend. Animals, and plants for that matter, aren't forced into a purpose—that isn't the way Creator works. It's more a volunteer system, where each creature seeks to serve in the best way possible. The first dog chose our purpose for us and we have been serving it ever since. Would you like to hear the story?"

"Very much so," Jane replied, stifling another yawn. "You don't mind if I close my eyes while I listen?"

"Not at all," Max said as he began his tale. "At the beginning of time, there was but a single language. Often Man, beast, bird, and flower would speak together around the great Council fires. Trees would bring messages they heard the wind whisper as it passed through their leaves, and wisdom was sought from the great stones. All things lived together within Creator's blueprint for life, and there was great peace.

"As time passed, Man, with his superior abilities to think and reason, began to use the information passed at these Council fires for his own benefit. He began to manipulate the Earth to suit his desires alone. He forgot to be thankful for what he took and began taking more than he needed. Before, when he gathered food, he would not take the first berries he found, but blessed them, sparing that first bush. He took only from the second and third so one would be left to multiply in the next season. Then he began taking all with great disregard. He took without thanking or consideration. Finally the Council of All decided that Man must be shown the error of his ways.

"A special meeting was called, and Man was not invited. Each part of creation sent one to represent them: one Deer, one Eagle, one Tree, one Snake and so on, until each spirit was represented. Each was given a turn to voice complaints against Man's behavior. It was at this Council that Man's fate was decided. He must suffer separation from all of nature until he could understand his actions as greedy and destructive.

"And so it was the next day, the Council spoke to Man of their decision. He was no longer to be a part of everything that was, or be able to understand the languages of his brothers and sisters in the plant and animal kingdoms. Man did not protest. By now his conceit fooled him into believing that he was wise enough and skilled enough to live alone. Man's refusal to defend himself sealed his fate. With deep sorrow the Great White Bear slapped the Earth with his paw and a crack began to form between Man and Nature.

"The Earth rumbled and the crack grew wider and longer, but Man's pride made him stand fast. He did not ask forgiveness as the crack grew into a gulley and the gulley into a wide gorge. He offered no word as the distance between himself and the rest of creation grew greater.

"Just before the gorge grew so wide it could never be spanned, one animal defied the council. At the last moment, the Dog sprang forward and jumped the gorge. He walked to Man, gently licked his hand and sat down beside him.

"The Council of All stood shocked at Dog's action. Finally Eagle spoke: 'Little Brother, have we not all decided Man's fate? Why do you stand beside him now?' Dog raised his head and stood proudly next to Man, saying, 'There must be one who will stand beside Man to protect him and remind him of the love he has lost this day. There must be one that will comfort him in his loneliness and urge him to return to us. I will be that one; this is the purpose I have chosen.'

"And so on that day, the Grand Canyon was formed and still remains a quiet reminder of man's separation from Nature. It was at that moment Dog became Man's best friend. It is the great hope to this day that Dog's gift of loyalty and love will someday spark the return of Man from his exile. In the end, it will be the dog that leads him home."

Several moments of silence passed between them as Jane took in the full measure of the story. "Beautiful," she mumbled. A solitary tear escaped her eye just before fatigue finally overtook her.

Max watched as she fell into a deep sleep. He glanced at the dying fire and with a sigh closed his own eyes. For the first time in a long time he allowed himself to relax completely. Jane was kind and good and more than a little off her path, but he could help her. His life had taken on its true meaning this afternoon. Tomorrow he would guide her forward as his kind had always done. He would be true to his purpose, and in the end, he would lead Jane home.

FIVE

...from this side of life, sometimes all we see are hard times and diappointment, but when we look at it from above, the beauty of the pattern emerges

Jane woke to bright sunshine and the smell of ashes. The fire had died hours before, and the chill of the autumn morning occupied the house. She yawned and rolled over to find a pair of chocolate eyes staring into hers.

"Good morning," Max said. "Did you sleep well?"

"Like a rock. I don't even think I dreamed," Jane replied as she pulled herself up, wrapping the afghan around her in a tight cocoon. She sat silently for a moment, letting her mind come to terms with being awake. When she had accomplished focus, she stood up to work on balance. "Chilly in here, isn't it?" Jane shuffled towards the kitchen, flicking the heat on as she went. Max was on her heels. She unlocked the back door, opened it and looked down at Max.

"Very considerate, thank you," he said as he trotted to the porch.

"I told you, I lived with dogs," Jane smiled as he passed.

"I can manage the screen door myself," Max said over his shoulder.

Jane heard it slam as Max pushed his way through. She went to the coffee pot and began her morning ritual. As the hot water slowly filtered through the grounds she made her way to the bathroom. *I am over these clothes—twenty-four hours in the same sweater is enough. A shower is going to feel great.*

Jane stared at her reflection in the mirror. She would practice what Max preached yesterday and look for all the ways she was wealthy. Starting with her physical appearance would be a good first step. Aside from the unicorn-like bump in the middle of her forehead, she had to admit that she liked what she saw. Long dark hair framed an oval face. Pretty, even very attractive if it came right down to it, and she let herself admit it. Dark eyes and full lips rounded out the face. Her skin was more olive than pink and she was trim, a perfect size eight, which suited her height. At five foot five she was well proportioned.

Jane stripped off her clothes. *I do like my looks. I'm lucky to be healthy and whole. I have a good mind that serves me well...when I use it. I guess this is wealth. I enjoy a wealth of health and that certainly does make my life rich.*

Hot water sluiced over her body, easing the sore muscles and scraped skin she gained from her fall. She grabbed the bar of Ivory and held it to her nose, breathing in deeply. The scent reminded her of the carefree days of her childhood when the world made sense and joy could be found in the simplest places. Jane let her mind take flight. *Children can find joy anywhere—in dewy grass, a hay loft, in scrambled eggs and pancakes, or a chance to play outside. Joy is anywhere their imagination takes them. To a child, the world is new and full of wonder, and awe is always waiting just around the corner. But adulthood sure has a way of blinding a person. We have a knack for allowing our everyday problems to cloud our vision and steal our ability to be constantly astonished by the simple act of living.*

Life is so much easier when you're young. It's all planned out for you. It has direction and purpose and clarity. You go to school to prepare yourself for your adult life. Each step is carefully structured for you; someone tells you where to go and what time to be there. The goals are clear. But when you finally graduate into your adult life, what is it that you really know?

Yes, you're good at learning, but who taught you how to think? Where are all the skills and tools that help you anchor your dreams in the real world? When you find yourself standing at the corner of "The Rest of Your Life" and "Welcome to Reality," and the only thing you can remember about navigating it is "don't take candy from strangers," it hits you. I don't know the first thing about who I am or what I'm doing here.

What you do understand with shocking clarity is the fact that the light is going to turn green any second and you have to step off the curb, but knowing that Lincoln was the 16th president or that 2/4ths equals ½ isn't going to help you much.

Jane wondered what Max had in store for her. She was so lucky to be having this experience, to have Max. She had been given a great gift. *I don't want to spend years in therapy to find out why I keep making the same poor choices over and over any more than the child of an alcoholic wants to become an alcoholic. I have to learn how to break the chain, take the reins of my life in my own hands. I don't want to wait until I'm fifty before I understand how life works and why I seem to allow others to decide the twists and turns of my path. I don't want to date the same guy in a different body, and have the same poor relationships time and again.* But Max was here to help with that. He was her guide and this felt like the first day of a brand-new school.

She decided she wouldn't try to control the day but allow it to unfold, let Max do his job. She had a million questions, but she was being gifted with a wondrous opportunity and she would give herself over to it completely, without expectations or demands. She would let go of the control she had been straining to keep for months and just go with it for a while, letting the experience take her where it would.

Jane braced her arms on the shower wall and let the hot water run through her hair and down her back. She watched as it twirled down the drain in a little whirlpool. Two days ago she would have found the drain another metaphor for her life, but today, with Max here, she felt real hope.

If she could get a sense of the purpose and meaning of life rather than the chaos and doubt she had been drowning in, then she could work through the rest. If there was a purpose, there had to be a plan; and if there was a plan, then someone or something knew what it was. Knowing that the universe has order and meaning would be enough.

There was a little pain in her heart as she thought back to all the plans she had when she first graduated from college, which included taking a job to support her life and writing beautiful books in her off hours. The picture in her mind included a spare little loft in the artsy section of Atlanta called Little Five Points that always smelled of oil paint and turpentine. The building would be colonized by other young creative types working on pottery, sculpture and jewelry, along with other writers like her. She would spend her free time in the company of the like-minded, reading experimental poetry and sipping lattés. The reality was not nearly as attainable as the dream.

Jane jumped at the first offer that came along from a newspaper in Atlanta. Although she had never lived in a city before, she justified the move as fate, her dream coming true. The plan had been to work a while, get her fill of city life, and when she was published, move to a rustic cabin in the woods, just like this one, where she could practice her craft in romantic solitude.

Reality set in the moment she landed in Atlanta. There was no artist's loft—the entrepreneurs of real estate had long since cashed in on that idea and converted them all to multi-million-dollar condos. What she could afford was a very vanilla two-bedroom, one-bath in a sprawling apartment complex. Her neighbors were no more artists than they were friendly and, on her salary, four-dollar lattés were a once-a-month treat. The arrow of her dreams had missed its mark. She had landed twenty-three miles north of the thrumming heart of the city in the sprawling suburb of Lawrenceville, caught somewhere between the well-manicured lawns of the American Dream and the road less traveled. Quiet and well-mannered, life there was like a steady diet of buttered toast. Comforting, predictable even, but constantly begging the question, "Where's the jelly?"

She hadn't known then how life could conspire to anchor one to a place with a chain of bills and responsibilities. She felt trapped in a lifestyle she never imagined could become more of a hindrance to her dreams than a springboard. Her job as a staff writer wore on her, and the stress of daily deadlines sucked away any energy to write the great American novel. After three years she didn't even have her own byline, and her writer's notebook yielded little more than fits and starts. Jane doubted whether she ever had the talent to do more than fix her own dinner or program the television remote. Maybe writing was her version of those adolescent fantasies everyone has, like becoming a rock star or scoring the winning touchdown in the Super Bowl.

What's worse, she was now painfully aware that she was stuck in a life she didn't want, and one she had solely created by her own choices.

The final blow came the day she was laid off. Her stomach had been knotted when the editor called her into his office. Circulation was down, blah, blah, people were cutting back to the Sunday edition, blah, blah. This is just temporary; we'll call you when the situation rights itself, blah, blah and blah. The life she viewed as dull and unworthy must have been looking back at her in exactly the same way because it rejected her as completely as she rejected it.

So if writing wasn't her purpose, what was? But then, that's what this month is all about—to find herself again, make sense of things and get back on track. She sighed deeply and hoped a month would be enough. She was running low on money, out of ideas, and faith in herself or anything else was completely gone.

Jane toweled dry and wrapped another around her wet hair. Steam billowed from the bathroom as she made her way into the bedroom to dress. Not knowing what the day would bring, she opted for comfort and utility, selecting jeans, a sweatshirt and hiking boots. She looked at her watch on the dresser. Max said to let time have its way in this, so she decided that while she was here, she wouldn't keep track of it or try to measure it. The watch would stay where it was. Jane quickly applied the blow dryer to her hair and headed for the kitchen and her morning coffee.

Max was waiting patiently by the screen door. She let him in and set about combining the perfect blend of sugar, cream and coffee while Max refreshed himself at the water dish. "So when do we begin?" Jane asked as she sipped from the cup.

Max looked at her and cocked his head. "This part of your journey began yesterday, or did you forget all of that while you slept?"

"No, I didn't forget," Jane corrected. "I just meant when or where do we begin again today?"

"First, you never really *begin again,* Jane, because you never stop,"

Max replied. "From the moment you're born you are on the path. You, like so many others, just fail to see the path or recognize it when it's revealed. If you imagine life takes place only in the exciting moments, you are missing a great deal. Life happens in the quiet moments as well, when you're alone. Rushing to create the next exciting moment robs you of the ability to enjoy and appreciate who you are and what you have been given already.

"We touched on this yesterday. Rushing from one high moment to another blinds you to your insight and deafens you to your own wisdom. You're too busy to recognize what you have accomplished and too wired to hear the voice within. It's at that moment you begin to lose your authenticity and start to measure yourself through the eyes and judgments of others. You become someone else's creation and no longer your own."

Jane looked down at her coffee. She felt a twinge of shame for speaking without thinking. Max was so right. She had better settle down and start taking this seriously. It wouldn't be just about the lessons; it would also be about the in-between time, when she could mull them over and make them her own. She might *understand* what they meant if she ran from lesson to lesson, but she would never really come to *know* if she didn't shift her thinking and her attitude. "Sorry, Max, I will try harder to be the student you deserve."

"I'm not your teacher, Jane; I am only your guide. I may know what to show you and where to find it, but what you make of it is entirely up to you."

Jane took a deep breath. "Okay, I understand. I mean, I know. Bear with me."

Max pulled his lips back from his teeth a bit in what seemed to Jane the doggy equivalent of a smile. "My kind has been bearing with you since the first dog jumped that ditch. I won't stop now."

Jane took a deep breath and concentrated on preparing breakfast. The urgency she felt to move on to the next adventure would have allowed her to barrel ahead without eating.

For any of this to stick, she would have to do more than just visit with an idea or concept, she would have to take the time to bring it home to live in her heart and mind. An action as simple as eating a bowl of cereal could bring the quiet minutes she needed to hear herself think.

Jane placed a bowl of kibble in front of Max. *This was one smart dog.* She took her own bowl and spoon, along with her coffee, and forced herself to sit at the table. Taking a deep breath and exhaling slowly, she began to eat. Her mind took her back to the occasions when she was alone and thought herself bored. If she had just used that time for a quiet walk, allowing her mind to empty itself of all the daily chatter, grocery lists, deadlines and "must do's," what would she have heard? Maybe her small still voice would have gotten the chance to whisper, "You aren't happy…This is not who you really are…Change your direction."

Jane was toying with her coffee cup when she realized that both she and Max were finished eating. She drank the last of her coffee and rose to put the dishes in the sink. Turning back to Max she said, "Okay, I'm ready now. Where to first?"

"You have the map in your head, Jane; you tell me what's first."

Jane sniffed, "If you're counting on me to know where to go, we are both in trouble. I've been trying to sort this out for months, and the more I try, the worse it gets."

"Then let's start with your questions again," Max said. "What were your first thoughts this morning?"

Jane pondered before answering. "In the shower I was thinking how much I would like to know that life isn't random chaos, that there is a master plan, some sense to it. I was also thinking about purpose, or rather, my purpose. Can I have faith that there is a purpose or destiny for me? I guess that would be my starting point."

"Okay, we have a map." Max fell silent, his brows knitted together in thought. Jane followed his gaze as he looked around the kitchen and fixed his eyes on the far wall. Hanging there was an old piece of embroidery in a homemade frame.

"Take that stitch-work down, Jane," he said. She followed his instruction, walking over to the wall and removing the frame.

"What do you see when you look at it?" Max asked.

Jane examined the piece for a moment. "I see a piece of needle-work. It says, *'I show you doubt to prove faith exists'.*" It struck Jane as familiar. "Hey, I know that quote, it's by Robert Browning." Jane loved quotes. She used them all the time, even in her work at the newspaper when she could find the appropriate place. Seeing this quote stitched on the sampler sparked the memory of another: *"The best days of your life are the day you were born and the day you figure out why."* It was the sum of all her questions and the reason behind her quest. She couldn't remember who said it, and she was usually so good about remembering authors, but the words haunted her. Why was she here? What was the point?

Pleased that she recognized the sampler's contents, she went on with her analysis. "There are words in the middle and they are surrounded by a border of fancy stitches." Jane flipped it over and then back. "There is no backing to the piece. The fabric is a bit tattered and there is a stain on the lower right-hand corner. It looks very old."

"Sit down and really look at it, Jane," Max urged.

She moved to the table and sat in the chair she'd occupied only a moment ago, holding the frame in both hands as her eyes moved over every corner, every stitch. *What does he want me to see?*

Max continued, "Shut your eyes for a moment. I am going to tell you the story of this particular piece of embroidery."

Jane did as Max asked and shut her eyes, lowering the frame to her lap. His voice took on a gentle, far-away quality as he began to speak.

"Imagine this little town years ago. Let the highways and billboards fade from your view. Instead of the stores you frequent, filled with all the lovely things you can buy, see them replaced with the wispy smoke of the farmhouses and cabins that once dotted the mountainsides. Close neighbors could be miles away, and any luxury you desired would have to be fashioned by your own hands. This is the way it was in the not so very long ago.

"Fathers taught sons the art of farming, butchering, hunting and—yes," Max quirked his brows, "even the making of white liquor. Mothers passed skills to daughters such as broom-making, basket-weaving and fancy thread-work, like tatting and embroidery. So it was when this mother and daughter stitched what you now hold in your hands.

"At the end of the day, when the chores were done and the meals finished, they would sit together by the light of a lamp and do fancy stitch-work. The mother would show the daughter a new stitch on her hoop, which the daughter would copy and practice. Eventually, hers matched the mastery of her mother's and a beautiful pattern would begin to emerge on a simple piece of cotton cloth.

"One day when the daughter came to the table she was crying. She had received news that the young man she fancied had met another girl and was planning to marry. The daughter was heartbroken. All her plans and dreams had gone up in smoke. Her mother tried to console her, but nothing brought the young girl comfort.

"At last the mother picked up the hoop her daughter had been working on and turned it upside down for her to see. 'Look at the work you have done. From this side you can see only the knots and a few tangles of thread. There is no real beauty in it. Now look at it from the other side,' she said, turning it over. 'All you see is a beautiful pattern. This is very much like the days of our lives.

"'From this side of life, sometimes all we see are hard times and disappointment, but when we look at it from above, the beauty of the pattern emerges. There is a pattern to life, even when we can't perceive it. It is not until the work is done that it becomes clear how perfectly our lives are lived.'"

Silence filled the kitchen, signaling the end to Max's story. Jane opened her eyes slowly, still caught in the spell the dog had carefully woven. She gazed down at the rugged frame in her hands and took a fresh look at the simple beauty of the needlework—each thread placed just so, all of them in positions carefully chosen to add to the whole.

She turned it over again and looked at the back. Indeed, there were knots and threads that crossed each other. Although the colors were there, the pattern was jumbled. She raised her arm and held the piece above her head so only the underside was visible. *This is how life looks to us,* she thought, *scrambled and twisted with no purpose.* Lowering the frame she then looked down on the beautiful design. *This is how life must look to God, a perfect blend, a magnificent fusion of living.* Jane looked hard at Max. He was silent, his brown eyes looking into hers, waiting for the point to hit home. When it did, she spoke in barely a whisper.

"I never thought of it like this, Max. We all understand that life can be chaotic and the events of our days can appear to be random, but wisdom comes from knowing—really knowing—there are reasons for everything and a meaning to each occurrence. And faith, true and abiding faith, lies in the absolute certainty of this."

Max smiled broadly and shook his head. "Yes, Jane, yes. The next time you face disappointment or grief, or get lost in the chaos of your life, remember you are seeing the tangled threads and knots that seem to be without reason. But from above, the many colored threads of our lives sewn together produce a beautiful pattern. There is a plan."

Jane wandered around the kitchen lost in her own thoughts. She washed her cup mechanically, folded the dish towel and straightened things on the counter, all the while mumbling to herself. "It's so simple—I never saw it before—but it's simple. You either know something or you don't. Either you have faith in God and know there is a pattern to life or you don't. All it takes is a grain of faith the size of a mustard seed, but when you don't have that grain, it might as well be a boulder. So every time I doubted myself and my life, I really doubted God. No wonder I lost my connection. I have been denying God in every doubt and choice I've made lately. Wow!"

Max interrupted her reverie. "Yes, Jane, it is you that chooses the threads of your life and where they are placed. That's what free will is, and God watches over the emerging pattern."

"God never abandoned me, did He, Max?" Jane looked at him misty-eyed. "I abandoned Him."

"The promise of free will was given to you completely and without exception. Even God can't intervene on your behalf without breaking His promise…*unless you ask*," Max said, putting the emphasis on the last three words.

"But I have been asking, I have been praying. He hasn't answered," Jane countered.

"Ah, you're waiting for the burning bush." Max shook his head. "I just don't understand the human species. How did you all drift so far away from who you really are? I have heard so many of you talking about getting back to nature, as if you could be separate from it in the first place. You act as if you can be outside nature, like an alien visitor to this universe, and you're not. You're part and parcel of it, as much a part of nature as a blade of grass or a...raccoon.

"For a species with such enormous intelligence, sometimes humans are as dumb as stumps. You're not any different than I am, Jane; you just have the illusion you are. What's worse, this illusion allows you to think you aren't connected to the divine, that somehow the Creator doesn't communicate with you all the time. You're choosing not to hear Him. You have this idea that He should come to you in a certain way when all the time He speaks to you through the things you are the most familiar with.

"Sometimes God waits in the hope you will find Him in your heart, Jane, and act from that discovery. Sometimes your answers come by other routes, like out of the mouths of family and friends. Answers can come in a song or a passage from a book, or even a sudden idea that you think is your own, when actually it's divine inspiration. But make no mistake, He speaks to you. He always has and He always will." Max snorted. "I would think the appearance of a talking spider and an almost angelic dog would be proof positive that God answers prayers."

"Yeah...it sure is," Jane whispered, looking down at the tips of her hiking boots. She felt silly and embarrassed.

Max got up from the floor where he had been lying and went over to her. He nuzzled his blonde head into Jane's hand. "Don't be so hard on yourself—we can all get lost in the dark."

They stood together quietly for several seconds...man and best friend. Jane absentmindedly scratched Max behind the ears and took the moment in. *This is peace,* she thought, *simple quiet peace.*

"Are you ready to find purpose?" Max said.

Jane wiped the moisture from her eyes. "You bet. Lead on, Mac Duff."

"I thought we agreed on Max," he joked, trying to lighten Jane's mood.

"It's an expression," Jane said sarcastically.

"Oh" was all Max uttered, shooting her a mischievous look as he trotted to the door.

SIX

...when an action or purpose brings you passion and joy, then you naturally follow it

Max took the lead once they were outside. Jane followed along breathing in the smell of the woods. It was a perfect, crisp fall day. The sky was Carolina blue and it seemed to Jane that even the sunlight was different. There was a crystalline quality to it, a new sharpness she had never noticed before. *Maybe the sunlight has always been like this and I just never noticed. If understanding and knowing are two different things, maybe looking and really seeing are the same way.*

Jane's reverie was interrupted by her cell phone vibrating in the pocket of her jeans. Checking the caller ID, she saw it was her boyfriend's number that showed on the screen. The whole purpose of coming here was to gain some private time and space; she'd explained that to him before she left. She'd been gone less than four days, and this was his third call. Irritated, she sent the call to voice mail.

"Are you okay back there?" Max called over his shoulder

"Yup, just appreciating the beauty of the pattern," Jane teased.

Max wagged his tail in approval. "Just keep up with me; we're going pretty deep into the forest."

"Okay," Jane shouted back, jogging to catch up with him. "Just remember you have four legs and I only have two."

They walked for a long time, chatting about the fall colors and trying to guess when the first snow would appear. Jane had never ventured into the backyard at the cabin, let alone hiked this far into the woods. Max slowed his pace for her when the trail got rocky or steep. They crossed the same stream a couple of times as it meandered and turned back on itself. One part of the path required a lot of ducking and holding tree limbs on Jane's part. The sun was high overhead, and Jane was out of breath and on the verge of asking for a time-out when they suddenly broke through the dense woods into a clearing.

Max stopped and sat down, ears up, looking straight ahead. Jane followed his gaze. She was learning to recognize his body language. The clearing was not as big as a meadow, but large for the forested area they were in. In the middle of the space was the largest oak tree Jane had ever seen. The trunk had to be fifteen feet in circumference. It was much taller than the other trees ringing the clearing, and its branches spread almost to the edges of the open space. The tree's leaves had changed into their fall attire, their colors so vivid they hurt Jane's eyes. Brilliant yellow at the top blended and faded into orange and orange into red and finally, the leaves closest to the bottom were still tinged with green. It was magnificent, and Jane wished she had brought her camera.

"There he is," Max said. "Grandfather Oak, the father of all trees in these mountains."

"You mean this is the very first oak tree ever?" Jane asked.

"No, there have been others before him, the ones that gave him life, but now he is the Grandfather and will be until his cycle is finished and another inherits his place."

Jane looked at the trees surrounding the clearing. It seemed they all grew in a perfect wide circle to honor the old oak and give him the space that his station demanded.

"The other trees know he's the Grandfather, don't they?"

"Yes, they do." Max smiled his doggy smile. "You're beginning to notice things, Jane, to really see."

Max walked towards the tree and Jane followed just steps behind him. When they reached the base, the dog sat once again and looked up at the oak. His tail was slowly wagging in anticipation. Jane stood rock-still and held her breath. Suddenly the oak's great branches began to sway as if a sudden gust of wind had come up—except there was no wind. They creaked and groaned with the movement, and as they did a rain of acorns fell to the ground, pelting both her and Max. Jane covered her head to ward off the onslaught and heard what sounded like a deep long sigh.

"Welcome, my four-legged brother," a deep voice boomed out. The sound startled Jane, causing her to jump back a bit.

"Hello, Grandfather," Max said. "It's been a long time since I've been here. It's good to see you again."

"And you" came the reply.

It took Jane a moment to get her bearings and take in the fact that the strange voice was coming from the tree. She was getting used to the idea that she could hear and speak with animals, but that her gift included plants and trees took a minute to sink in. She hardly had her mind wrapped around this before the voice came again.

"How may I serve you, Little Brother?" Grandfather Oak asked. The timbre of his voice was deeply bass, and he spoke more slowly than Max or Jane. It was exactly the kind of voice one would imagine an enormous tree to have.

"I have brought someone to hear your wisdom," Max said. The oak's branches swayed again, as if the tree were trying to get a better look at Jane.

"A human, I see...It has been a long time since any of the two-legged kind has sought wisdom from trees. I thought they had forgotten us. This is a good thing. Perhaps things are changing, Dog," the great tree said.

"Perhaps they are," Max answered.

"What do you wish of me, Little Sister?"

Jane's voice wavered when she replied. "Well, I, umm...I would like to know about purpose...*My* purpose, to be exact."

"What is your purpose?" the tree asked.

"I...I'm not sure anymore," Jane said.

Grandfather's branches shifted abruptly. "If you are not sure, who is?"

"Well, I always thought we came into life with some sort of fate or pre-ordained destiny," Jane said, regaining some of her mental balance.

"No one knows your purpose but you, my friend. Your purpose in this life is exactly what you wish it to be. No one picks that for you. You can choose to serve life however you wish. Where does your passion lie?"

Jane began to focus totally on Grandfather Oak. "My passion, the thing I love to do best, is writing."

"Then writing is your purpose."

"It can't be that easy," Jane said with a tinge of frustration in her voice.

"It is that easy."

Silence fell in the little clearing. *I must not be asking the right question or asking it in the right way.* The great oak sensed her confusion. There was a rush of leaves as the Grandfather cleared his throat and said, "What is it you wish to experience in this life of yours, Little Sister?"

Jane took a moment. "Well, I would like to write a bestseller, have a husband and children...I would like to—"

"No, this is not what I ask," Grandfather interrupted. "Those are all things you would like to *have*. What would you like to *experience?*"

Jane was in total confusion. She didn't know the answer to the question that the old tree asked. Her face blushed as she felt more and more self-conscious. She knew the great tree felt her discomfort and so did Max.

"Remember your currencies," Max whispered out of the side of his mouth.

"Ah, okay," Jane mumbled. Max was easing her back on track. "I wish to experience love, passion, fulfillment...I want to feel like I am making a difference in the world. I want my life to mean something, stand for something. Let's see...I want to be secure and have peace in my life and joy, great joy."

"Yes, those are wonderful experiences, good choices," Grandfather said. "You see, you may or may not have the things you desire in life, like a husband or a bestselling book—these things are up to you in the getting of them. But you cannot base your state of being in the world on whether or not you get them. You may marry and have offspring, but what if you don't? Would you still wish to experience joy and fulfillment?"

"Yes, of course."

"Then before you seek to *have* things, *be* the experiences you wish. In other words, be passionate, be fulfilled and be joyful. You must not count on things or even others to complete your life. Nothing and no one can bring you joy or passion. The source of those states of being must live within you. They must be a part of who you authentically *are,* apart from what you *have.* It is better to be complete first and bring the states of being you wish to feel to the rest of your life. Then you will always be joyful and passionate and fulfilled no matter what comes to you or what fades away."

"Yes, I understand," Jane said. "What you're saying is, if I am happy and full of joy by myself, then no matter what happens in my life, I will always be able to be happy and full of joy."

"Exactly. And what is it you do that brings the most joy and happiness to you?"

"Writing. I am happiest when I write." Jane smiled. She was catching on. "But what if writing brings me the most joy and I'm no good at it?"

Grandfather's branches swayed gently. "When an action or purpose brings you passion and joy, then you naturally follow it. You practice it and enjoy the practice. It brings the states we speak of to you because you are equipped to do it well. You never dream of what you cannot do. When you love something, you will pursue it, cultivate it and become skilled at it. Success will follow."

Jane thought for a moment. All that Grandfather Oak was saying resonated as truth, and yet she hardly saw this practiced in the outside world. "I know lots of people who aren't living their purpose. I know one girl in particular who loved art, and she painted beautifully, but she was in the education college and graduated as a teacher. She makes good money teaching history now, and her life is settled and secure."

"And her states of being, what does she express?"

Jane thought about her college friend and bells began to go off in her head. "The last time I saw her, all the girl did was complain about her class, the kids and the school administration. She talked about finding a guy, getting married and having some kids of her own so she would have an excuse to stay home."

"So she was unhappy and unfulfilled, searching for a way to change her life?" Grandfather countered.

"Yes. I never thought about it at the time, but looking back, I see that she was miserable."

The Great Oak continued, "Misery and unhappiness is currently her state of being, and she will carry that over to her mate and her offspring. She will look to them to make her happy. It will become their job, and that is a large task to ask of anyone, especially a child."

Jane could see his point clearly, but life demanded more from one than just happiness. "Yes, but you also have to be practical. What if she had followed her art and never made any money? Not only would she be miserable, but she'd be broke too!"

"She lacked confidence in her talent and doubted her ability. When you find your purpose and you practice it with intent and imagination, you will flourish. Not everyone can paint, not everyone can write, not everyone can build a house. Others depend on you to bring your gifts to them, just as you depend on them to share their talents with you. Would you have given money for this girl's work?"

"Yes, she did beautiful work; I would have loved to own one of her paintings," Jane said enthusiastically.

"Then you make my point," Grandfather replied. "Humans must learn to bind their intellect together with imagination, creativity and intuition. You think these traits to be flights of fancy, when in reality they are the very things that allow you to mold your purpose and your dream of life into something that provides you with abundance. Perhaps this sister would have been happier teaching art."

It seemed so obvious to Jane. *Why didn't she choose to teach art instead of history? Yes, at that time there was a great need for history teachers so her profession seemed secure, but what did she give up for her security?* "It can't be this simple," she said.

"It is that simple if you wish to experience simplicity. If you wish it to be complicated, then you will choose those things that will complicate the matter. It's your choice," Grandfather Oak announced. "Tell me, little one, what are you writing now?"

Jane shifted uncomfortably. "Well, right now I am not writing... I mean, I intend to write, when I get my life straightened out. I have, well, complications that worry me, so I just can't concentrate at the moment," Jane stammered.

Grandfather chuckled. "Stop choosing complicated. If the best expression of joy and fulfillment to you is to write, then write. You are not feeling joy or fulfillment or peace because you are not doing the one thing that brings these feelings into your life. For goodness' sakes...write! The expressions of self and the experiences you wish to have must burn bright in your own heart before you can bring them to others. Allow yourself to become abundant and complete from the purpose you have chosen."

Jane walked in a little circle, running her hands through her hair. *Again, that simple,* she thought. *If I want to be happy, I have to do the things that make me happy and only then will I be able to pass happiness on to someone else.* She recalled the choices that had led her to this point in time. *Perhaps I should have given my other currencies, like joy and fulfillment, as much weight as I gave the making of money. I wonder how my life might be different now. Maybe my relationship with Dan would be totally different if I had been complete before we met.* Jane became aware of the creaking of branches and the rustling of leaves as Grandfather Oak spoke again.

"Come here, Sister, and hold out your hand." Jane walked closer to the tree and held out her hand. A branch slowly lowered itself in front of her and dropped a tiny acorn in her palm. "Is this the seed that grows into a mighty oak tree?" he asked her.

"Yes," Jane replied quickly.

"Look again," requested Grandfather.

Jane gazed at the acorn. Time passed as she again struggled to comprehend what the great tree was asking her. Finally she spoke. "My answer is still yes. All acorns are destined to become oaks."

A long sigh came from the tree. When he spoke again, his words were strong and to the point. "Will this seed—as you hold it in your hand—grow into a mighty oak?"

Jane looked down at the little brown seed, and a smile of understanding crossed her face. "The answer to your question is no. This seed in my hand is not the beginning of an oak tree."

"Hah!" boomed Grandfather. "Good answer. The seed of meaning and fulfillment grows in all of us, Little Sister. All acorns have the *potential* to become great oak trees, but the *seeds* of the oak, as those of your purpose, must fall on fertile ground. This seed, if kept in your hand, will never become a tree. It must be planted in fertile soil and receive the rain and the warmth of the sun to sprout. So it is with your chosen destiny, my human friend. Know that it naturally lies within you and is waiting to burst from its tiny shell. Just like the oak tree, you must plant your purpose in the soil of your heart and tend it, nurture it, so the gift inside can grow.

"Each of us is born with our own brand of purpose and greatness. It lies inside us, waiting to be discovered and nurtured. Each of us is born with a gift or passion that serves the world. It is this passion, tended and grown, that will blossom into purpose, fulfillment and abundance. It is up to you, Little Sister, to explore the depths of your own internal forest and find the seed you have been hiding so long. Seek it earnestly, for many of your kind pass away without ever realizing their greatest gifts. Within its shell is the potential to express your purpose and your destiny. When you find it, cherish it, for it is at the center of a life well lived. This is all the wisdom I can give you today." And with that Grandfather Oak straightened his branches and fell silent.

Jane stared at the tree for a moment. "Thank you so much for giving me this insight. I won't forget."

The giant tree stood quiet and unmoving.

"We should go," Max whispered.

Jane had been fixed so intently on the acorn and Grandfather Oak's words, she had forgotten Max was there. She slipped the acorn into the pocket of her jeans, and in silence she and Max turned and left the clearing.

The trip home was quiet and didn't seem to take nearly as long returning as it had coming. Jane supposed it was because her mind was still with the tree, even though her feet were on the path. It was only when the cabin came into view that the quiet was broken like a magic spell, and easy conversation between Max and Jane began again.

Jane pushed the back door open; she never locked it, not here. In the city she locked all the windows and doors. She locked her car when she was in it and when she was out of it. It wasn't a comfortable habit for Jane, always needing to be on the lookout. It spoke to her of fear. For her, the city was definitely not a place that promoted security or happiness, and yet she'd found it so easy to ignore her own preferences when she moved there. Then again, she hadn't bothered to figure out what she really wanted. She had settled for what came her way instead of insisting on those things that would make her life all she desired.

No, the city wasn't her place in the world, and she wondered now how she didn't know that about herself. There was a lot she needed to discover about herself. Apparently many of her missteps and problems stemmed from not knowing who Jane really is.

It was past noon and both she and Max were hungry so she busied herself in the kitchen. Once food and drink had been accomplished, Max stretched out on the porch for a good nap and left Jane to her own devices. She settled in the chaise and looked out on the landscape of the backyard, deep in her own internal landscape as well.

If there was to be a purpose to her life, a destiny, then she alone was responsible for sewing the pattern. It would be determined by the choices she made and the actions she took. Those choices should be guided by what she knew about herself, except they weren't. She hadn't paid attention to what the inside of her was saying; instead she concentrated on how the outside needed to appear. Jumping at the newspaper job read well on her resumé, but it wasn't writing, not the kind she wanted anyway. Living in the city seemed like a great adventure at the time, but it was really trading sirens and horns for birds and breezes singing in the trees.

In an effort to appear to be a writer, I have chosen those things that would distract me from actually writing. The kicker is: how can I write about comfort, love and meaning if I don't have them inside me to give? So what do I want to experience in my life? What states of being do I treasure most?

Jane ran into the house and picked up a pad and pen. She returned to the chaise and made a list of all the ways she wanted to feel. She wanted to be happy, to be loved and love in return. She wanted peace, joy, security, abundance, meaning, and a sense of fulfillment—those would do for the moment. As time went on and she excavated more of who she really was, her authenticity, she would no doubt add to the list.

Jane looked each choice over again. None of what she had done up to this point would bring her those things. Not in the way she wished to experience them. In fact, she had been doing just the opposite, in the misguided hope that something or someone would give her what she really wanted. She silently wondered how many people in the world had done the same thing. How many people drifted into a life just because it looked like the normal and accepted way to go about living, or because their parents wanted it for them, or maybe because they just didn't take the time to figure out what *they* really wanted? How many were living the consequences of those choices just as she was right now? Jane supposed there were lots of folks out in the world wondering, *"How did I get here?"* and blaming husbands, mothers, bosses, and even God for dreams that never came true.

We choose the threads and the colors in the tapestry of our lives, whether we are conscious of it or not, Jane thought. *The master plan on Earth is about free will and the choice to create whatever pattern we wish. God is watching a million—a billion beautiful patterns emerge every day, and if the knots and threads are scrambled and the pattern not so beautiful, it is the doing of human beings. Each of us is responsible for our own piece of the whole and, perhaps, even for those pieces of our brothers and sisters, for when part of the whole is flawed, the whole of it is flawed.*

Jane felt an energy run through her that she had never felt before. It was glorious and terrifying at the same time. If her life were to have meaning and purpose, she would have to plant the seed of it and be responsible for its growth. It wouldn't be Creator's or anyone else's fault if it lay dormant inside her and never blossomed. It was up to her and how scary was that? Now that she knew this, how would she go about making it all happen?

SEVEN

...it isn't a one-size-fits-all proposition

Max interrupted her internal quest with a loud yawn and a full-body stretch. His legs stretched out rigid and stiff, and it was not until he relaxed that he opened his eyes and scanned the porch for Jane.

"Oh, that was lovely," he said. "Nothing beats a good nap. How long have I been sleeping?"

Jane smiled at him and threw her feet off the chaise to face him directly. "I have no idea—an hour maybe. Max, while you were asleep I've been doing my homework. It's no wonder nothing in my life is going the way I want it to. I have been putting the cart before the horse. I haven't been driving the bus—life has. I've been so busy running from one life event to another I never stopped to figure out if what I was doing actually supported what I wanted. I wonder if any of us connect the dots between our actions and our dreams."

"So all of this is helping you make sense of your life?" Max asked.

"Yes, a million times yes," Jane answered. "We're doing this backwards—I mean approaching life backwards. We run after the material things in life in the hope that a thing or person will make us happy and complete, when all the time we have no clear idea what happiness means to us. It isn't a *one-size-fits-all* proposition. For example, the city may be the definition of happiness to one person, but for me, happiness is being here. And if I know what makes me happy, then I truly am the master of my destiny and can become my own guide."

"Sounds like an *I-am-my-own-grandpa* type of thing to me," Max snorted sarcastically.

"Oh, come on, be serious, Max," Jane pleaded. "I'm getting it, aren't I?"

Max's eyes softened as he looked at her. "Yup, sister, you're getting it!"

Jane smiled, pleased that the wisdom she was receiving was not lost on her. "Okay, but I'm stuck on something. When Grandfather Oak and I were talking about my friend who taught history, he said we needed to use our intuition and imagination to create work we really love. I understand it, but the world, as we've set it up, demands you do things to support your life and pay your bills. I don't think I would have the confidence to strike out on my own and create sources of income with my writing. What if I couldn't do it?"

"Okay, so we went two steps forward and one step back," Max said.

"What do you mean?"

"You get the purpose part, and the potential, but as far as translating and anchoring it in your real life, you're still a bit fuzzy. You can't be afraid of your talent and expect to develop it. The act of doubting yourself and your potential is what stops you."

"Okay, explain it to me."

"Better yet, I will take you to someone who can explain it far better than I ever could," Max said.

"Great, let's go! I'm ready." Jane stood up quickly.

"But he isn't," Max replied.

"I'm not following you, Max," Jane said impatiently.

"It's not time for him to be at the spot we meet. I usually visit with him in the afternoon."

Jane heaved a deep sigh and sat down again. "What time will we go then?"

"Again—slow down, Jane. You're still trying to rush from one exciting moment to the next. Give this all time to sink in. Enjoy it and be grateful for how far you've come. Notice yourself in this moment. Be aware of your thoughts as your wisdom takes root and makes itself present in your life."

"I just want to make sure I have enough time to understand all you have to show me," Jane said.

"If you slow down, so will time, and you will never run out of it. If you zip along from one big thing to the next, you will miss the quiet valleys of peace where true knowing is born. Savor each experience in the moment of its happening and feel each feeling fully."

Jane thumped her pen nervously against the paper. It was just that morning that Max had warned her about rushing her life, and yet here she was still pushing. This was all so exciting and her brain was in high gear. She was just becoming aware of all the possibilities in life. A door was opening, and who wouldn't want to press on as fast as they could?

"Have you thought about what I asked you to think about?" Max asked. "Have you thought about all the wealth, joy and happiness you already have in your life?"

"Not exactly...I started to, but so many things have been

happening and I—"

"Take this time until we leave this afternoon and think about it. Say a little prayer of thanks for all you have at this moment. Thankfulness and gratitude play a large part in the way you look at your life. If you don't take the time to be grateful for what has already appeared, how will you ever know the value of anything? Do your homework. You can't build a strong house on a weak foundation and expect it to last."

"Max, again, you're right. I haven't given it enough thought. I think I will find a spot right now and count my blessings."

"Don't forget to include in those blessings the fact that you had the presence of mind to know you didn't like your job and to recognize that the relationship with your boyfriend was failing. These were urgings from the deepest part of you—messages. Even though you weren't able to connect the dots between awareness and action, awareness is the first step. And don't forget to say thank you for being laid off or taking the fall you took on the steps of the overlook," Max reminded her.

Jane looked puzzled. "Those weren't good things, Max. Those were bad things. Am I supposed to be grateful for the bad things too?"

"It's your perception that those things were bad. They all led you here, to this moment, didn't they? If any one of those things hadn't happened, you wouldn't be here now."

Jane put her head in her hands and fingered the bump on her head. If she hadn't hated her work, she probably would have done a better job and might not have been laid off. If she hadn't been laid off, she would never have had the time to come to the cabin. If she hadn't come to the cabin, she would have never stopped at the tourist overlook and fallen. If she hadn't fallen, she would never have met Grandmother Spider, Max and Grandfather Oak, or experienced anything else that may follow, for that matter. All of it had to happen in a certain way, all the events aligning at the perfect time to bring her to this point. It was all part of her tapestry, a series of threads woven to produce *her* pattern.

Jane ran her hands through her hair as she looked back at Max. "I see…I can look at all that's happened and see how I perceived those events as bad. I didn't recognize how each was a step that led me here. But you're right, Max—if any one of those things hadn't happened, I wouldn't be here now."

"Exactly," Max said. "The things you label as bad—the accidents, the misfortunes—may be the very things that lead you to find the good. You prayed for help, Jane; how it comes and in what form is not for you to decide. Divine intervention has its own perfect timing. Your job is to have the faith to know that answers will come; stay aware and recognize them when they show themselves. What seems like a terrible occurrence today just may lead to your greatest success."

Jane was silent for a moment. She was experiencing so much, and for the first time her precious talent for words seemed to fail her. "I think I will go to my bedroom and mull all this over. I have some catching up to do."

"Go ahead. There are few things better than a little alone time. I'm content right here," Max said as he rolled onto his side and closed his eyes. "Just leave the door open and I'll come get you when it's time to leave."

Jane made her way to the bedroom and flung herself on the bed. Her mind ran back in time, examining the connecting paths, random choices and high points of her life. She traced disappointments and failures to new opportunities and successes that had never before seemed to have any connection at all. There were times when Jane considered herself merely lucky, but now with clarity, she could see how all the disjointed pieces of the puzzle fit together. *Everything happens for a reason and there definitely are no coincidences. There is a whole lot more going on in life than we know.* Suddenly Jane felt sorry for anyone who hadn't been hit on the head, figuratively or literally.

As Jane began to catalog all the new blessings she was discovering, her cell phone went off. Grabbing it from the nightstand, she saw from the display that it was Dan again. *This is what makes him so good at his work, his dogged persistence. If I didn't know better, I might think he missed me.* Understanding his need for control and order, Jane knew this constant attention meant he viewed her as a loose cannon that needed a firm mooring.

She'd have to take this call if she were to have any peace at all. She stared at the phone, letting it ring several times before answering.

"Hello," Jane answered, trying to sound casual.

"Hey, it's me." Dan's voice echoed in her ear. "How are you?"

"Fine—no, make that great. So much has happened, I doubt you would believe me if I told you."

"Good. Is it enough to make you come back?"

"Not yet. I'll probably need the full month." Jane wondered if he missed her or if he missed the idea of her being there. Before she could ask he went on.

"You're actually planning on staying the full month?" Dan whined into the phone. "I would have guessed you'd be sick of your own company by now and heading home at the end of the week. Jane, you're out of a job. What could you be doing up there that's so much more important than looking for work?"

Jane held her breath. She wanted to tell him that she was really enjoying her own company. She wanted to tell him about Max, but refrained. Jane hated confrontation. It was a weakness she often hid behind—not speaking her mind or saying what she really wanted shielded her from others' disapproval. She was the girl who just went along with everything. When others had definite opinions and ideas, she kept her mouth shut and acquiesced. It made her feel spineless and mousey, and yet she hated the idea of arguing. No wonder Dan seemed overbearing and self-centered. As far as he knew, she had no real preferences or desires of her own. He had his way in everything, even when it was to her detriment.

"Jane? Are you still there?"

"Yeah, I'm here."

"I just asked you a question. Do you remember Mitzi Shallowford?"

"Mitzi...Isn't she the little blonde friend of yours who works for a vanity press?" Jane felt a pang of jealousy.

"Yes, that's her. She told me there may be an opening for an editor where she works. You should come home and look into that."

"Dan, I want to *write* books, not edit someone else's."

The conversation continued back and forth, Dan insisting she would be better off back in Atlanta looking for work, and Jane stewing in passive-aggressive silence on the other end of the line. After ten minutes of Dan's logic and a healthy dose of scolding, Jane was at her wits' end.

"Dan, I'm not coming home now. I have some important things I have to do. I don't want Mitzi Shallowford to get me a job, and I don't want to listen to you tell me what I should and shouldn't do right now. If you can't understand and support me in this, then don't call me again."

Jane's mouth dropped open at her response. She had never spoken to Dan like that before, and the hush on his end spoke of his surprise. Several seconds later she heard the tiny click through the receiver indicating that he'd hung up. Part of her reveled in her newfound voice; she had finally stood up for herself. If life was hers to create, then she needed to start drawing some boundary lines. At the same time, the other half of her was terrified she might never hear from him again. Jane shut her eyes for a moment and wondered about the consequences of the conversation.

She was scared. She had left Dan for a month fully intending to return and make the relationship work. If he left her, who would she be then? Her fear was overridden by the words of Grandmother Spider and Grandfather Oak. This was her life and she had to be acting like it. Jane sighed deeply. It was too much to think about now. Max was probably right—a good nap might be just what she needed. She couldn't control whatever decisions Dan would make; she could only make her own. Accepting those terms, she let herself drift off to sleep.

How long she slept, she didn't know. The morning's hike and the emotional phone call had taken their toll. She was dreaming about a princess in a high stone tower besieged by a dragon. Jane could feel hot dragon breath on her face as she awoke to find Max's snout pressed to her nose.

"Time to go" was all he said before trotting out of her room.

EIGHT

...give your doubt nothing to feed on, and it will die

Jane slipped into the bathroom, rinsed her face and combed her hair. She wondered if she should change her clothes. "Can I go dressed like this?" she shouted.

"Sure," Max called back. "There are lots of vacationers in town, and the lifestyle here is very casual."

Jane stumbled down the hall, still groggy from her nap. "Where are you taking me?"

"I'm taking you to see a friend of mine. He's a human like you," Max answered as he headed for the door.

"Will we need the car?"

"Yup, it's too far to walk." Max went on, "Before I came to you, this man and I spent our evenings together. I bet he's wondering what's happened to me. Every day he takes his dinner at the little café on the edge of town. Then he sits a while on a bench in the park. We can meet him there."

"He's human?" Jane asked incredulously. "You speak to him too?"

She made a grab for her purse and car keys lying on the counter.

"You're not the only human who has taken this journey, Jane," Max said, looking over his shoulder. "There are others. Some don't need a rap on the head, because some are gifted with the ability to see the oneness. It makes it much easier if you don't judge how you think the world should be and what's possible."

"Ouch," Jane said. "You don't mince words, do you?"

Max climbed in the passenger seat of the car and threw her a smile. "I don't mean to be harsh, Jane, but the truth is the truth, and more often than not, it doesn't take a whole lot of words to speak it. There is power in truth, and sometimes when we hear it, it can feel like a slap in the face. Really it's just the power in the words spoken that hits home."

Jane smiled back at Max. "I'm getting sick of saying *you're right, Max,* so I'm just going to say okay on this one."

"Aw." Max stuck his head out the window as Jane turned the car towards town. "That's too bad, because I do like the sound of *you're right, Max…*It has such a nice ring to it."

Jane drove slowly, listening to the radio and singing along when she knew the words as they wound their way towards the little mountain village. When they passed the scenic overlook, Jane slowed the car and wondered what Grandmother Spider thought of her conversation with Dan. *How would she write it, as an ending or a new beginning?*

After another mile or so Max said, "We're getting close. I can smell the café."

Sure enough, around the next curve in the road stood a small square building surrounded by a gravel parking lot. A hand-painted sign over the door advertised home cooking. Just as Max had said, it was on the edge of town. The left-hand side of the parking lot boasted the end or the beginning of an asphalt walkway. The restaurant was clean and well tended; one could tell it was the gathering place for the year-round residents. No doubt the owner's family had deep roots in the history of this area.

Jane eased her SUV into the lot and found a parking space at the side of the restaurant. After she let herself out, she went around to the other side of the car and opened the passenger door for Max.

"Why don't you go in and order something to take home, Jane," Max suggested. "The food is great here, and you probably won't feel like cooking when we get back."

Jane took a deep breath; it sure smelled good. *It's no wonder Max could tell we were close.* The air screamed of fried chicken and fresh biscuits. "Good idea."

"And you might want to buy a pack of cigarettes," Max added.

"Cigarettes?" Jane shot him a puzzled look. "I don't smoke cigarettes, Max."

"I know," Max replied. "But the man I am taking you to see is a Native American elder. He is part of the great Cherokee people that once called much of western North Carolina, northern Georgia and part of Tennessee their home. It is tradition when you meet and ask something of an elder, you gift them. Tobacco is a sacred plant to the Native Americans. When you give him the cigarettes, it's a sign of respect, and he will know you are serious about what you're asking and that you value his wisdom."

"Okay," Jane answered. She left Max on the front porch and went in to order. The interior of the restaurant was homey and quaint. All the available wall space bore hand-painted murals that reminded her of the primitive style of Grandma Moses. They appeared to be scenes from the local countryside. Jane couldn't help staring. A pleasant round woman greeted Jane from the counter.

"My daughter done those," she said, beaming with pride. "She's only a sophomore in high school, but she can paint like nothin' you ever saw. Her teacher says she's gifted."

"She certainly is…They're just beautiful."

The woman extended her hand to Jane. "The name's Ida, but you can call me Cookie—everybody else does."

"Okay, Cookie, my name's Jane," she said, taking the plump hand in hers. "I'm staying down the road, and your food came highly recommended to me. I thought I'd try it."

"Well, that's fine. It's all home cookin' and the best in these parts," Cookie replied, taking out her pen and order pad. "Down the road, you say? The only place down the road that's empty is the cabin by the big curve in the road—that the one you mean?"

"Yes, that's it," Jane answered, smiling. Local gathering spots were gristmills for gossip. She knew her presence would be a juicy tidbit for the next day or so, at least until someone's wife left him or some other scandal made her old news.

"Well, how nice." Cookie went on, "That's been empty for a long time now. I always said it could be a pretty little place with some tendin'. It's a shame to have it just sittin' there all dark and sad lookin'. I see you've took up with Goldie." Cookie switched subjects without so much as taking a breath. She nodded towards the door where Max was waiting. "He's been a regular here for quite a while— comes around of an evening for the leavins' of the day. Some of our customers save him a scrap or two from their plates. He's such a friendly thing; we'd wondered what happened to him."

"Yeah," Jane replied, glancing at Max, "I'm a sucker for strays." She left the conversation there but secretly wondered if any of the other customers spoke with Max. She placed her order and told Cookie she was going for a walk in the park and would pick the food up in an hour. She asked for a pack of cigarettes, and after making her purchase she headed back outside. Max took the lead and headed for the path. The entrance to the park was only a few feet from the car.

The park was more a slender trail through the woods than the manicured meadows you think of when parks come to mind. The footpath was about three feet wide, bordered by another foot that looked to be maintained by a weed eater rather than a lawnmower. Beyond that margin, the forest grew in a riot of native plants and trees. Every couple of yards there were little green signs lettered in gold identifying the flower or bush growing there. Most of the plants were past blooming, but still, Jane was surprised to find many of the bushes vibrant with berries and fall color. It wasn't until Max broke into a lope that she noticed a bench on the trail ahead and resting on it, an old man.

He was nut-brown and his slightly rounded shoulders hinted at his age. His face showed cracks and wrinkles like a well-worn saddle, and his long steel-gray hair was pulled back in a ponytail. The hands that protruded from his worn shirtsleeves were thick and spoke of years of hard work.

Jane walked at a normal pace. She wanted to give Max and his friend a minute alone. The two were obviously happy to see each other. The old man clapped his hands together when he saw Max coming, and a wide smile split his face. The moment Max reached him they seemed to melt into one thing. There was such an unruly mix of flannel shirt and golden hair it was difficult to tell where the man ended and the dog began. Jane knew Max was anything but a normal dog, yet at that moment he was like any other, all paws, fur, tongue, and tail.

Jane felt a pang of jealousy as she approached the bench. Since Max had shown up at the screen door, she had been so caught up in the odyssey she was living that she hadn't realized how her affection for the dog had grown. He had never greeted her with such warmth, and Jane realized she had no idea how Max felt about her. He seemed to be well known by the café crowd and particularly fond of this old man. So much so, she wondered why he hadn't found a home among the people he knew. For the first time the thought crossed her mind that she might be just another temporary stop for Max. When he had done all he could for her, he would move on and out of her life. Before she could feel the full impact of what Max's leaving would mean to her, she felt a gentle paw on her leg, breaking her chain of thought.

"Jane, this is Jacob; Jacob, this is Jane," Max said as an introduction.

She managed a smile as she extended her hand to the old man. "Jacob, I am so glad to meet you."

There was no traditional handshake. Jacob took her hand lightly in his and held it steadily as he looked directly into her eyes. Jane felt he wasn't so much looking *at* her as he was looking *into* her, and for a long moment she felt awkward. His sharp eyes showed none of the milky tint that came with age but were a clear deep brown almost as dark as Max's. His gaze was sharp yet held a twinkle of humor. When he finally spoke, it was to Max. "Huh, I should have known your absence would be explained by a pretty female," he chuckled. "I just thought she would be four-legged." Max threw his head up and down snorting.

"Here Jane, come and visit," Jacob said, sliding down the bench to make room for her. When Jane had seated herself the old man didn't angle his body towards her as one might when holding a conversation but sat facing straight ahead. Jane took a cue from his posture and sat as he did, straight ahead. Max sat directly in front of her.

"I see you are a special friend of Goldie here," Jacob said. "I can only assume he brings us together for a reason."

Max interjected, "I do, Jacob. Jane is a seeker and I have volunteered to guide her in that search. Her questions are of a particular nature, so naturally I thought of you. By the way, I've chosen a new name. Jane didn't think Goldie suited me, so I chose Max."

"Ah…Max…Max…I like that name. Okay, Max it is."

Jane glanced at Max. He shot a look at the pack of cigarettes she was holding and then back at Jacob. She cleared her throat and offered the tobacco. "As Max said, he has been my guide on this very…unusual expedition. I have a question he feels you will be able to answer for me. I've brought you this gift as a token of my appreciation for your time." Jane looked at Max to check her approach to the matter at hand, and he nodded a slight affirmation.

Jacob took the cigarettes from Jane and put them in the breast pocket of his shirt. He folded his hands together interlacing his thick fingers and placed them in his lap. Closing his eyes, he said, "I will do what I can."

Max looked back at Jane and she guessed it was her turn to speak again.

"I went to see Grandfather Oak to talk about purpose. I am confident of who I want to be and how that blends with my purpose, but I still have doubts about whether I can do it well."

The old man tilted his head down until his chin almost rested on his chest. He sat stock-still; his only motion was his slow deep breathing. Seconds turned into a minute, and one minute stretched into two. He was quiet so long that Jane wondered if he had even heard her, or perhaps he'd drifted off to sleep. She glanced at Max; his eyes were fixed on the old man's face in anticipation, so Jane continued to wait. When at last Jacob broke his silence, it startled Jane so much she jumped. His tone was reverent and even the cadence of his speech changed.

The old man pronounced each word distinctly, as if each carried great weight and therefore demanded honor for its expression. In a modern culture where slang and slur melted one word into another, it seemed as if the concept in a sentence was enough. When Jacob spoke, the beauty of each word was given its due. Jane was caught in an ancient spell long cast by all the wisdom keepers and storytellers through the ages.

"There is a sacred cave hidden deep within these mountains not far from where we now sit," Jacob began. "If you visit this cave you will see the symbols and markings of a people that lived and thrived in this area long ago. These symbols and markings are stories and messages left by a powerful Medicine Man as a record of his wisdom and teachings for those generations that would come after his passing from this Earth. It was here that a young Cherokee boy learned the lesson of the wolves within us.

"Long ago when these hills belonged to the First People, this boy possessed a great thirst for knowledge. He wished to learn all he could about everything his eyes beheld. He also wished to know how to become a human being.

"You see, *being* is easy. You are a being at the moment of your birth, but becoming human is hard. Unless you strive to become human you will never be humane, nor will you experience humanity in its fullest.

"And so it was this boy wished to become a great human. He longed to understand love, compassion, mercy, forgiveness—all aspects of the highest vision we hold for ourselves. In the natural way, if a thing that is good exists, the opposite of that good also exists. For every day, there is a night; for every summer, there will also be a winter. In this boy's journey to discover and live these good qualities, he also found the bad: hate, indifference, cruelty, and blame.

"To his sadness these opposites lived inside of him. He could be kind and thoughtful in one moment, and the next moment he could be cruel and inconsiderate. Hard as he tried, he could not seem to overcome his opposites. Though he asked many, none in his village could satisfy his need to know and understand himself. Finally he knew he must seek this wisdom outside his community. And because of his burning desire to be a great human being, the young boy set off to find the Medicine Man and the cave in which he dwelled.

"The search was hard, his travel long, but after some time he found the holy Medicine Man and asked for his help. Boy and Sage sat in front of the fire that night and talked of things great and small until at last the boy revealed the question that had brought him to this place.

"'Grandfather,' he said, 'within all brothers and sisters, there are things that are worthy of being and living, but also things that are not. It is my truest wish to become a great human being, one worthy and wise enough to lead my people. How can I master those unworthy things and only express those that are worthy?'

"The old man sat in silence for many long minutes and finally spoke. 'There are two wolves fighting inside each of us, my boy—one is good and the other evil. Which one will win the battle?'

"The young boy pondered, thinking hard on the Medicine Man's question. He thought throughout the night and the next day as well. He walked the forest while he searched his heart for the answer. He prayed to the dawning sun that he might solve the riddle. He listened to the wind and spoke to the water, but no answer came. At last, when he had exhausted himself and all his resources, he returned to the cave and the Medicine Man.

"'I do not have the answer,' he said. 'Grandfather, if there are two wolves fighting within me, one good and one evil, tell me which one will win?'

"The old man replied, *The one you feed.*'"

Jacob lifted his head and opened his eyes. He waited for several moments before he spoke again. "This is as true for good and evil as it is for confidence and doubt. For each positive emotion we feel inside us, we also carry the opposite. The one that wins the struggle for dominance will be the one we feed well. Give your doubt nothing to feed on, Jane, and it will die. Serve only your confidence and it will grow strong within you."

Jane had fallen into the rhythm of the conversation and waited for what she felt was an appropriate amount of time before she replied. "Jacob, that was a wonderful story; it helps me understand the constant internal battle that seems to be with me all the time. I guess I'm not alone—all of us humans must also suffer with the opposites. The trick is not to constantly weigh confidence and doubt, good and evil—or love and hate, for that matter. Instead pick the one that serves our vision of who we want to be and feed that choice. If we feed that vision, the opposite will fall away."

Jacob nodded his head once in affirmation. "To feed the best in you is not a selfish act, Jane. You will be surprised how well it serves others when you serve yourself first. You cannot be at your best when your heart is timid and full of doubt."

"Thank you for all you've told me today. I hope Max and I can come back and visit you often," Jane said as she stood.

Only then did Jacob face her. He gave her a mischievous wink and said, "Next time, bring something sweet. I have a big sweet tooth."

Max and Jacob said their goodbyes and then Jane and Max started back down the path to the café. Nothing was said until they reached the parking lot. "Thanks Max, meeting Jacob was great, not to mention comforting. At least I know for sure I am not the only one who hears you speak. I did feel a bit awkward a couple of times; he took so long to answer me, I thought he'd fallen asleep."

Max shook his head and replied, "Jacob was raised in a culture much different from yours. When you ask him a question he has great respect for both you and the question. He believes you deserve the best answer he can give you, and that doesn't come without some thought."

"Wow, I never thought of it like that," Jane said. "In my world if someone asks you a question and you don't immediately have an answer, they think you don't know or you're lying."

"Do you feel you got the best answer possible?"

"Yes, it was perfect; the story was wonderful and easy to understand."

"Then you learned two good things today: the care and feeding of a wonderful life and how to serve others with respect." With that Max trotted across the porch of the café and sat beside the entrance.

Jane went inside to retrieve her take-out meal. Cookie inquired about her walk as she slipped another small aluminum-wrapped parcel into the bag. "Just a little somethin' for Goldie," she said. "Give him a good scratch behind the ears for me."

It was dark by the time she and Max got back to the cabin. The little breeze of the afternoon had become a gusty wind, and Jane shivered as she opened the kitchen door. She hadn't told Max about the "leavin's" Cookie had sent for him, and he was delighted when his dinner included a couple pieces of chicken-fried steak and a biscuit covered in sausage gravy. His tail wagged furiously as he spoke kindly of Cookie. For the second time that day, Jane felt a little jealousy bubble up in her chest. She really didn't know much about Max, and with all he was doing for her, she felt a bit guilty. Aside from his role as her guide, she felt great affection for him. To her, this relationship should be a two-way street, and so far it was all about her. Tonight she would ask him about his life and maybe discover the reason for the sorrow lurking just behind his eyes.

NINE

...sometimes in life, logic loses its wisdom to the longing of the heart

Jane transferred her fried chicken from the styrofoam container onto a ceramic plate and plopped herself in front of the fire she'd lit only moments before. To Jane, the word *home* always conjured up images of good food, family and a warm crackling fire. Tonight was no different. The west wind had brought with it a cold rain that beat thickly against the windows, but the glow from the fireplace held the storm at bay. The cabin seemed to wrap its wooden arms around Jane and Max, keeping them safe and dry. It had been too long since anywhere felt like home to Jane, and she took a moment to enjoy the complete and utter contentment she felt now. There was nowhere she would rather be and nothing she would rather do at this moment than be right here with Max. Jane felt very wealthy indeed as she shut her eyes and let gratitude compose her silent prayer.

This is what Max meant by letting time have its way. These are the moments between one life event and another when you can stop and appreciate how far you've come and where you are now. These little valleys of quiet bring with them the opportunity to feel thankful for the experiences in our lives. They are moments of reflection when you can look around and measure what you've created in your life so far—precious pools of time when you can see how every decision and every action you ever took led to exactly this moment.

Jane glanced over at Max lying inches away from her outstretched legs. He was gnawing on another bone and seemed as content as she.

"Max, what would you be doing on a night like this if you weren't here?" Jane asked.

"I would be under a porch or a rock ledge somewhere riding out this storm."

Jane reached up and placed her empty plate on the end table. "I don't understand. So many people know you and seem to really care for you—why haven't you found a home with one of them? Jacob clearly adores you."

Max shifted around to face her. "Yeah, I am pretty fond of him too, but it wouldn't work with Jacob. He has…*cats.*" Max almost spat the word.

Jane giggled. "What happened to the oneness you talk about— aren't cats part of it too?"

"I didn't say they weren't," Max said a bit defensively. "But I have preferences just like you do, and I prefer not to live with them. They have way too much attitude for me."

Jane was still giggling. "I know plenty of dogs that live with cats and they really seem to have genuine affection for one another."

"I know, and frankly I don't understand the appeal," Max replied as he shot her a stern look. "But it's my preference. You prefer living in the country to living in the city, don't you?"

"Okay, touché." Jane read his look and didn't press the matter. She grabbed a pillow off the couch and stretched out on the floor so she could watch the flames of the fire. She had wondered about Max and his life all day, and the chance to ask him had finally arrived.

"How did you come to be here anyway?" she asked. "Were you born in the wild?"

"No, I was born in the city. Macon, Georgia, to be exact."

"How did you get here?" Jane inquired.

Max folded his front paws with the same hint of sadness there Jane had seen before touching his face. He stared at her for a moment, deciding whether or not to answer. With a long sigh he looked into the fire and began. "I was born in the fall, weaned and ready for a new home around Christmas. I was a present for a family with three small children. The papa brought me to my new home on Christmas Eve with a big red bow tied around my collar. I felt very special and as excited as the children when they saw me. Every dog dreams of having just one child to run and play with, and I had found a home with three. I felt like I'd hit the jackpot.

"We lived in an apartment so there was no private yard to run or play in, and the kids and I certainly had more than enough energy to wreak havoc in the five little rooms we called home. We had a good mama and she took us to the park every day. That was heaven—to roll in the grass, bark as much as I wanted and play with the ball we couldn't throw in the house. Still, we had more energy than the couple of hours in the park could drain away, and although she tried, Mama couldn't keep up with the messes we made." Max looked down at his paws. "I guess I was a handful then, what with the housebreaking and the chewing.

"The children were too young to walk me by themselves, and Mama had to do it while Papa was at work. It took a lot of time to get three children and a dog ready to go for a walk three or four times a day. She tried, but even at my young age I could sense that three kids and a new puppy was just too much for Mama to handle.

"There was much discussion between Papa and Mama about what to do and how to handle the situation. They felt bad because they'd let the excitement of Christmas overcome them and really didn't think the whole pet situation through well enough at the time. Many people don't think it through, by the way. They really want a companion but give little consideration to size of responsibility, and it usually ends in tears and heartache, like it did this time. Finally it was decided that I would go to Mama's sister and her husband. They had no children, but they did have a house with a yard."

"Well, that must have been better; at least you had a yard to play in." Jane turned on her side and reached out to stroke Max's head. He seemed so unhappy remembering the past, and she desperately wanted to comfort him.

"It was for a while. They were very kind and fussed over me so I would feel welcome. They bought me a little house of my own and put it in the backyard close to the back door. I really enjoyed it and settled in, determined to be the best watch dog and friend I could be. Part of being a good dog is taking the time to learn what your human companions need and want. The kids came to visit a lot at first, but after a while, they came less and less and soon I only saw them on special occasions.

"But the man and woman were professionals, so they both worked during the day. It was a bit difficult for me to really get close or be affectionate with them. I didn't see much of them, just in the morning and at night when they came home. They taught me in-house manners and how not to jump on guests or people I met on the street. I was a quick study and I believe that pleased them.

"They were a busy couple and liked to travel. Not too many hotels allow dogs, and I became just another inconvenience, a detail they had to deal with before they could enjoy their lives. So arrangements were made for me to go to yet another home. This time I was given to the boy next door, Tom. He used to feed and care for me while my people were gone and I knew him quite well.

"Tom was in college in Atlanta and lived in a fraternity house. I guess he thought I would make a good mascot, so at the end of summer, off we went. I was a bit concerned about moving so far from home, but all the boys accepted me with open arms. The house was very big and always smelled of dirty socks and stale beer. There was something going on there all the time. I could hardly tell who lived there and who didn't, so guarding the place was a nightmare. It didn't take me long to figure out that the boys didn't care who came and went. In fact, the rule of the day was the more, the merrier, so I concentrated on learning what being a good mascot meant. I must have gotten it right because the boys gave me my very own bandana with their Greek letters on it. I was very proud of that."

Max looked at Jane, his face so pinched with grief it almost broke her heart. "I'm sure you were the very best mascot any frat-house ever had," Jane said, still stroking his shaggy head.

"I believe I was," Max went on. "By that time I'd grown into my purpose and tried to be a best friend and companion to Tom and all the other boys." Max was silent for a moment, his brown eyes staring into the flames. Jane knew he wasn't seeing the fireplace, or her, but rather looking into the windows of his past.

"It was a good time in my life, perhaps the best so far. Lots of Frisbee and football; the boys were outside a lot and liked to rough-house. I had all the exercise and freedom any dog could want. I developed a real taste for pizza while I was there—pepperoni is my favorite. There were lots of back scratches and plenty of affection to be had. I learned the rhythm of the house. Up early Monday through Friday and sleeping in late on Saturday and Sunday mornings. Tom left his closet door open, and since most of his clothes were on the floor of his room, it became my private sanctuary. I used to curl up in there when I wanted a quiet nap. The frat-house was truly a home to me.

"I really loved Tom and felt he loved me back. I slept on the foot of his bed most of the time, unless he was entertaining and then I took the living room couch. Summer breaks back in Macon were a welcome change of pace, and I got to see the couple I had been with before. That was nice. I felt like I fit, belonged somewhere and served my purpose...*until.*"

Jane cringed when she heard him say the word "until." She had seen him relive those fond memories and even smile a bit when he mentioned pizza, only to have the happiness replaced with the same old sadness. She didn't speak; she let Max choose his time to continue.

"The beginning of the third year I was with Tom, he met a girl. She seemed nice enough, but she didn't like to touch me or have me rub up against her clothes. She definitely didn't like the fact that I slept on Tom's bed when she wasn't around. I sensed Tom had chosen a mate and that he was happy. I was happy for him and tried very hard to make it easier for the girl to like me. I thought at first she was afraid of me, even though I could sense no fear from her. I tried to be gentle and calm, but each time I approached her, she backed away and made a face. As hard as I tried, she wouldn't warm to me. As time went on, when she was with Tom, it was like I didn't exist for him. Sometimes he even forgot to feed me. The more time he spent with her, the less he spent with me.

"At Easter, he decided he would move in with her. They rented a tiny apartment on the other side of town. I didn't like the idea of moving and leaving the other boys, and I didn't have fond memories of what apartment life was like, but I trusted Tom would make it work for all three of us. I guess I misjudged my bond with Tom and his bond with the woman.

"A week before we were supposed to move, she gave him an ultimatum. It was either me or her. She didn't want me living with them, said I was messy and a bother and she didn't want dog hair on everything she owned. They argued a lot over me. I could tell it was tough for Tom. He tried everything he could to find someone to take care of me, but he only had seven days. The boys at the frat-house, the ones I had been so faithful and loyal to, wouldn't or couldn't take me. Friends that lived off campus would have taken me, but their leases didn't allow pets.

"Soooo, one day we went for a long ride, up here to these mountains. He drove around for a long while and then pulled over at the very same scenic overlook where you fell. We got out of the car and he petted me a while. Just him and me, sitting there looking out at the mountains. Finally he hugged me very hard, wished me luck and told me I would find another family in no time. Then, he got back into his car and drove away. I didn't chase him, although I wanted to…I knew he was making his choice. Even though it broke my heart, I just sat there and watched his taillights until they disappeared."

The haunted look on Max's face did Jane in completely. She squeezed her eyes shut but the tears escaped anyway, sliding down her face. She could see him so clearly, sitting in the parking lot, watching the car pull away—his heart breaking as he struggled to understand his abandonment. She thought she had composed herself enough to speak, but her emotions betrayed her and she let out a little sob when she tried. "I…I'm so sorry that happened to you, Max. I just can't imagine how you felt. How could anyone do such a thing? You might have starved to death. Why didn't he take you to a shelter where you could have been adopted?"

Max pulled out of his memories and came back to the present as he recognized the sadness in Jane's voice. "He tried the shelter route. He called one, but it was full. He didn't pursue it any further because time was short and he was getting a lot of pressure from his girlfriend. I did hear him say he thought my chances of getting adopted were slim since I was fully grown and therefore not as desirable as a cuddly puppy." Max tilted his head to one side and shot Jane a coy look, batting his doggy lashes at her several times. "He was wrong, though—I am not without my considerable charms." His comical attempt to lighten the mood fell flat on Jane.

"Oh, hey, it's not that bad," Max continued as he inched his way towards her. He had traded the position of the comforted for that of the comforter. "I'll admit I was sad for a long while. But as time passed, the grief lifted and I made my way. I made friends with the restaurant owners and I didn't miss too many meals; they fed me pretty well. Up here there's lots of space to roam and plenty of places to find shelter. I learned a lot too, Jane, from Grandmother Spider, Jacob and all the plants and animals that live here, things I might never have known."

"I just can't understand how Tom could do that," Jane sniffed. "Who could just leave someone they professed to love behind—just drive away without so much as a backwards glance?"

"You'd be surprised. It happens all the time. With such close proximity to Atlanta, these mountains have become the waste receptacle for all the pets that have outgrown their homes or whose human companions have outgrown their interest in them. Dogs, cats, ferrets, even tropical birds and snakes are dumped here when their humans feel bored with them or overburdened. I've taken a few under my wing and helped them adjust. Some do quite well, while others die quickly from a cold winter or a broken heart. The hardest part for all of them is trying to understand why."

Jane fought to pull herself together, wiping the tears away with the sleeve of her sweater. She wished to be an ear for Max, a confidante, someone he could be himself with; instead he was, as he always was, her guide and guard.

"That's a hard story to hear. Don't you ever get lonely?"

"Yes, sometimes, especially on nights like this, I'm lonely. There are times I wish I belonged somewhere, but one thing I've learned, Jane: I would rather be lonely once in a while than live with someone who doesn't really love me."

Jane drew in a sharp breath. Max's comment hit home. Her boyfriend's image jumped to her mind, and she wondered why she was clinging to a relationship doomed to failure. "I think I'm about to learn that lesson myself."

"Really?" Max replied.

Jane chuckled. "Well, I thought I had found Mr. Right, but apparently I'm not Miss Right. I have a boyfriend back in Atlanta—well, have or had, at this point I don't know which tense would be correct. His name is Dan. I met him at a club through someone I worked with, which should have been my first clue, but he is really handsome and has a great job, so I started dating him. Everything was great for a while and then it began to fall apart."

"What happened?" Max said as he laid his head on part of Jane's pillow. He would be the witness to her story now, just as she had been to his.

"I was new in town—new job, new apartment, a whole new life.

I didn't understand then that it wasn't the life I wanted so I threw myself into it. I hadn't made many friends other than a few people at work, and one day when we were all in the break room, we decided to go out for a couple of drinks. We ended up at one of those clubs where you go to dance, meet people and drink, with the emphasis on drink. It wasn't a place you would go if you were looking for a relationship that lasted more than one night, if you know what I mean."

"Not exactly," Max said. "I've never been to a club, but I can imagine from the things that used to go on at the fraternity house. There were a few regular females, but most came and went."

"Pretty much the same thing," Jane went on. "I saw this guy staring at me and mentioned it to one of my co-workers. It turned out she knew him and introduced us. At the end of the night I gave him my phone number, and much to my surprise, he called me. We hit it off pretty well, started dating regularly and before long we became a couple. I guess I was so glad to have a boyfriend I glossed over the fact that there were lots of things about Dan that didn't fit me. I suppose I should have seen them as red flags. Maybe I did and just ignored them. Anyway, after we had been dating a couple of months he asked me if I wanted to move in with him. He had a wonderful apartment, and making the rent in my tiny place was a struggle. I don't know what I was thinking, but I accepted the offer."

Jane got up and threw a new log on the fire. She poked at it absentmindedly as she went on. "From the start he was more of a roommate than a mate. He was always going to play basketball or going out with friends after work. Not that I minded him having his own outlets or friends, but you would expect he might have included me in his nights out, or we would have made plans together more often.

"We talked about our dreams when we first started dating, and you would think the connection would deepen after we started living together, but it didn't. I feel like you should help your partner achieve their dreams. I mean, if you love someone, you want them to accomplish what they want in life, realize their goals. Dan doesn't seem to take my writing seriously. He thinks it's cute, but a pipe dream." Jane put the poker back in its place when she realized she was stabbing the wood more than adjusting it. She went back to her spot on the floor and the shared pillow.

"I'm an easy-going person, game for just about anything, but everything was Dan's way. If we went out to eat, he picked the restaurant. If we went to the movie, he picked the show. I know I probably should have spoken up more, but I learned not to very quickly. It was his way or nothing at all, and I really don't like arguing. I don't know, Max—it just seems we aren't well matched.

"Things have been going slowly downhill, and my response has been to try harder. I've turned myself inside out trying to please him. I used to sit alone at night and guess at ways I could make him see the real me. Nothing worked. He's started staying out later, and a couple of nights he didn't come home at all. I suspected he was seeing someone else, but I didn't confront him. I just…tried harder. I think he enjoys the convenience of me making his dinner and washing his clothes but honestly, I feel more like his mom than his girlfriend."

Jane shut her eyes for a moment taking in, for the first time, the full measure of what she had just related to Max. Hearing her story from her own lips forced her to confront the truth that had been stalking her. "Max, I don't think I have ever been lonelier in my life than when Dan is right beside me."

"Is that why he isn't here with you?"

"Yes. I needed to step back and take a look at our relationship without him present. But he's only a part of the reason I'm here. I just wanted a little time to get my thoughts together, see if I could figure out how to put my life back on the right track."

"Are you sure he's the right mate for you?"

Jane cocked her head to one side and sat silently for a minute. "A week ago, I would have guessed this was somehow entirely my fault. Now I don't know. Part of it could be me, part of it could be him, and maybe it's just us together. Maybe we don't fit. I don't know, Max… It seems like I've been so stupid about my choices in the past few years."

"You aren't stupid, Jane," Max challenged. "You were doing the best you could with the information you had. That's all any of us can do until we learn more, grow more, wake up to the way life works and begin to make better choices. You have a thirst for life, to learn and experience things—otherwise you wouldn't be on this journey… It would never have come to you. Do you really think you could be happy with half a life or half a love?"

Jane felt her eyes welling up for the second time. "No, Max, I don't want half a life or half a love." Her tears spilled over her cheeks and she lifted her hand to wipe them away.

Before she got the chance, Max sprung to his feet and said, "Don't do that."

Jane froze, her hand halfway to her face. "What's the matter?"

"Let the tears fall into your hand. Everything has a purpose and a story to tell, especially when the message comes from within you. Let your tears tell you their story."

Jane sat up and held her hand underneath her jaw. She waited for the tears to make their slow tracks down her face and drop into her hand. "Now what do I do?"

"Ask them why they came; let your tears tell you their story."

Jane looked down at the tiny puddle in her hand. She had never spoken to tears before, but firsts had become the norm of her life these days, so she spoke: "If you have something to tell me, please reveal it now."

Jane and Max watched as the liquid shivered and reshaped itself into one large perfect teardrop. It caught the firelight and reflected a prism of color within it. Jane felt like she was holding a perfect diamond in her hand. The tear expanded outward as if taking a deep breath and then it spoke. Its tiny voice sounded as clear and crystalline as the tear itself.

"Long ago there was a village in the place where this town now sits. As villages go, this one was large. It is not unusual in life that two will compete for the company of the same person, for it has happened throughout the ages. In stories told around the campfires, it was not unusual to hear of two men vying for the hand of a particular woman, or two women competing for the favor of one man. In this village there were two young maidens that loved the same man.

"But this is not the story of those two women or which one succeeded in winning his heart. This is the story of the tears they cried as each pursued him.

"Sometimes in life, logic loses its wisdom to the longing of the heart. The wanting of a person or thing can be so great, we are blinded to whether this person or thing serves us in the highest manner. Sometimes the prize looks so wonderful we abandon all we are and all we can become to win it. It was in the meeting of tears, shed by two such women so very long ago, that the real lesson lies.

"Once along the road in heaven, two tears were traveling. The first was traveling from the east, the place of innocence and youth. The second tear came from the west, the place of wisdom and experience.

"After a time of traveling their separate roads, they met and recognized each other by the sorrow that lay within them both. The tear from the west asked the tear from the east, 'Why were you shed?'

"The tear from the east took a long moment, gathering herself to speak. Finally she said, 'I am the tear of the woman who loved him and lost him. But tell me, sister, why were you shed?'

"The tear from the west sighed, and a knowing look passed through her eyes as she spoke, *I am the tear of the woman who got him.*'"

With that, the little orb began to spin in a circle and then dissolved in Jane's hand. Jane gasped and shot a look at Max. His eyes were bright when they met Jane's. "You gotta love it," he said, wearing his doggy smile. "You gotta love the magic in the world."

"I do, Max…I do." A little chuckle began to grow in Jane's voice. "You know what else, Max?"

"What?"

The chuckle burst into a full-throated laugh that pulled Jane's body into a ball. "I do feel sorry for the girl that gets Dan."

TEN

...the truest wisdom and the highest actions do not spring from the mind but are born in the heart

Morning found Jane and Max curled up together on the living room floor. At some point during the night Jane pulled the afghan off the couch and covered them both. The rain storm from the night before had calmed to a constant drizzle. Stretching and yawning, the two went through their usual morning routines. Max went outside while Jane showered and dressed. They reunited in the kitchen for breakfast and to plan the day.

Jane waited by the door as Max shook his wet coat on the porch. When he had gotten as dry as possible she let him inside.

"I know it's sloppy outside, but I love rainy days," Jane said. "It inspires me to bake. My mom and I used to bake on rainy days; I think that's why I love it. We'd fill the house with the aroma of chocolate chip cookies or brownies and all seemed right with the world. I think that's what I'll do—bake chocolate chip cookies and a batch of brownies. I already have all the ingredients; I bought them the day I got here. I was planning on a lot of alone time, and for that you need major comfort food."

Jane opened and closed cabinet doors looking for the bake-ware. "The only problem is having them around. Whenever I have sweets in the house they seem to call to me from the counter top. I end up eating way more than I should, and a girl has to watch her figure."

"You could give some to Jacob," Max said as he circled a spot on the kitchen rug and lay down. "He told you to bring something sweet the next time we visited. I don't think he worries too much about his figure."

"Great idea." Jane hummed as she busied herself with measuring spoons and mixing bowls. Her mind wandered back to last night's conversation as she worked. "Hey Max, last night we talked about what brought us here. You seem to have accepted Tom's leaving while I on the other hand keep trying to work things out with Dan. When do you know it's time to call it quits?"

"When you feel sad or guilty or resentful more than you feel happy and contented and there doesn't appear to be a way to fix things, you can be pretty sure it's time to move on and grow. I couldn't speak to Tom like I can to you, so there was nothing I could do."

"I'm asking because it feels like I am the one trying to make the relationship better. Dan just bulldozes along, and I trail behind gathering the pieces. I feel smothered by him, and other times I feel like I'm grasping at straws."

"You must see something between you two to continue to try," Max quizzed her.

"I don't know if I see something or if I just don't know who I would be without him. I think I have a big fear of being alone. I'm twenty-four and the clock is beginning to tick. I would like a family."

"If you don't know who you would be without him, then you

don't really know who you are in the first place. Being alone may help you find out. You can stay with Dan and feel smothered and grasping every day of your life from now on, or you can let go and make a space for new possibilities."

Max looked on as Jane mentally weighed their exchange. He knew she understood what he was saying, but it wasn't hitting home. Her *prove it to me* nature wouldn't let her take in the full measure of what he said. His eyes lit on the ten-pound bag of sugar sitting on the counter with the other baking ingredients. "Jane, I want you to dip your hands, one by one, into that bag of sugar and fill each hand as full as you can."

Jane gave him a puzzled look but hauled the sugar bag over to the sink and did as he requested. When she had two heaping handfuls of sugar, she glanced back at Max.

"Now leave one hand open, cupping the sugar gently, and with your other hand make a fist."

Jane did as she was instructed. She closed her fingers around the sugar, making as strong a fist as she possibly could. Sugar spilled from either side of her clenched hand.

"Now open your hand and tell me which hand holds the most."

Jane opened her right hand to find much of the sugar missing. "The left hand definitely has more."

"When you smother someone or hold on to them too tightly, the result is the same. You're hoping to keep what you have, but the reality is you lose most of what was there. It's the same with the spirit, Jane. If you squeeze too tightly, little of the original remains. Much of what the person is…disappears. In the end, you have almost nothing."

Max watched as a light went on in Jane's eyes.

"So while Dan is trying to change me, and I'm trying to hold on to him, we're actually squashing the spirit out of each other, making each other less than who we really are as people."

"That's a distinct possibility."

Jane emptied her hands of the sugar and turned back to her baking. She didn't say any more and Max let the conversation lie as it was. The problem was hers to mull over, and the choice was hers to make.

Once the cookies were finished, she moved on to brownies; and by lunch time, the dishes were done, the kitchen was tidied, and the counters bore several plastic containers of goodies. Max silently watched all the activity, dozing off and on.

Jane fixed herself a bowl of soup as Max retrieved last night's bone from the living room. All through her culinary efforts she had been thinking of Dan and the situation. "Max, do you think I could be addicted to crisis?"

"What do you mean?"

"I mean, do you suppose I create problems and make mistakes because I love the drama of it all?"

"Do you like the way you feel when you have problems?"

Jane crumbled a handful of crackers into her bowl. "No, I don't like the feeling at all. I worry all the time. It makes me unhappy and full of fear."

Max grunted. "Sounds awful—how could anyone like feeling like that?" His eyes went blank as he turned to his own thoughts. "I think humans as a whole don't recognize the signals they get when they make a choice. They don't recognize the signals so they just forge ahead into situations and circumstances that are troubling to them."

"I don't understand, Max. What signals?"

"Feelings, Jane, your emotions. Since we were talking about you and Dan, let's stick with that as an example. What did you feel when you first began your relationship with Dan?"

"Hmmm..." Jane thought for a moment as she swallowed a mouthful of soup. "I felt apprehension and excitement, hope and doubt, all at the same time. I felt like things were moving way too fast, but then again, they say when you find the right one, it just clicks."

"Are you clicking?"

"No."

"What are you feeling now?"

"I feel confused, unhappy...again, smothered. I suppose there are healthy doses of jealousy, anger and resentment thrown in there too. I never feel like he thinks I'm good enough. It's like he wants to remake me."

"Those are your signals, Jane. Something isn't right. Those feelings, your feelings are sending you messages. They'll keep coming until you take care of the source. If you don't pay attention, then you will spend the rest of your life feeling them over and over."

"Yes, but maybe it's my fault. Maybe I'm wrong and Dan's right and I should just change my ways."

"Then you wouldn't be Jane anymore, you would be Dan's creation. There's nothing wrong with you, Jane; it's just not what Dan wants. Dan is not what you want either, or you wouldn't be getting the signals you are. Look—nothing exists in the world without a meaning and function behind it. Nothing is random. Your emotions were given to you for a reason, Jane; they didn't just come with the physical body as some useless bonus."

Jane shut one eye and pulled her mouth to the side, straining to understand. "Explain all this a bit further." She got up from the table, crossed the floor to the sink and rinsed off her soup bowl and spoon, stacking them in the drainer.

"Better yet, if you're not afraid of getting wet, I will take you to the expert on emotions."

"I have a rain jacket and I'm sure I won't melt," Jane replied. "I'm game if you are."

It took no time at all for Jane to locate her slicker and rubber boots. In less than five minutes she was once again trailing Max through the backyard and into the woods. Under the canopy of the forest, the drizzle became more of a persistent drip than a steady rain. Even though there was no direct sunlight, the forest floor looked greener than Jane had ever seen it. The wet plants and bushes seemed to gain intensity, and Jane thought she had never seen so many shades of emerald in her life. The rain on the leaves gave them a waxed look and deepened their autumn colors. It was like walking through some fairy cave filled with sparkling gems.

Max was leading her on the same path they had taken on their way to Grandfather Oak, but instead of crossing the stream this time, they followed it, keeping it on their right. Jane chattered to Max in easy conversation as she concentrated on her footsteps. The leaves had begun to fall from the trees and were slick with moisture; the last thing she wanted to do was take another fall. With her luck she would see the same doctor she had when she first fell a couple of days ago, and Jane didn't know how she could explain yet another injury.

It wasn't long before Max and she began to descend a gentle slope. The creek became a series of small waterfalls laughing their way down the hill. Using trees for support, Jane made her way down to level without slipping. Max laughed as she thanked each tree for its help, but Jane didn't mind a bit. She felt differently about trees now. She knew each was a living spirit sharing her world instead of merely decorating it.

"Never hurts to be courteous or grateful," she reminded him.

"That's good. It means you are noticing, expanding your awareness of the life around you."

It wasn't only the trees that Jane felt differently about, it was everything. She took care to step on the barren earth rather than trampling the smaller plants along the trail. She was learning to listen, and as a result, she heard more. The background sounds of scampering squirrels or crackling twigs no longer passed by her unnoticed. The forest was not quiet, but alive with the music of living.

Smells also caught her attention. Everything had its own odor. Wet leaves smelled different than dry leaves, and even a stone had a steely mineral smell when wet. Jane felt her vision had changed, become more acute, enhancing colors and shapes. Her life was taking on a new richness and depth. She never understood how much she was missing by not taking the time to really see or hear, and she quietly wondered if she had been tuning out God in much the same way.

A quarter of a mile of level hiking brought Max and her to a small pond that formed a cove for the larger lake beyond. The water's edge was rocky and dotted with ferns and moss. Not too far away from where the water met the land stood a mature weeping willow. It was tall and straight and the branches hung full around it like long thick tendrils of hair. Max walked up to the tree and greeted her.

"Grandmother Willow, how are you this rainy day?"

"Dog, what a nice surprise. Lovely to see you here again," the willow spoke. The sound of Grandmother Willow's voice was soft on Jane's ears, like the sound of your mother's voice when she was tucking you into bed at night, calm and comforting. "Who is your friend, my dear?"

"This is Jane. I've brought her to you so you can tell her about feelings and emotions."

"Ah," the tree replied. "It would be my pleasure to share my story with her. Won't both of you come under my branches and shelter

113

yourselves from the rain?" With that, the slender drooping branches parted like a green curtain to make way for Jane and Max.

Jane didn't hesitate to walk under the branches into the natural clearing beneath. Under Grandmother's flowing arms the earth was covered with spongy moss, soft and remarkably dry. When the branches closed behind her, Jane felt like she was underneath some magical green cup, hidden away and protected. When she and Max were settled, the tree spoke again.

"So you have come to hear about emotions and feelings."

"Yes, I would like to know more about feelings as signals or messages. I know everyone has feelings, but I never thought of them as having a significant purpose."

"Oh, indeed they were designed for a grand purpose." Grandmother Willow went on, "They were created to be an internal guidance system, like signposts that tell you when you are on the right path and when you aren't."

"And weeping willow trees chose the purpose of being the keepers of the understanding of emotions?"

"Yes, Jane. I see our Max is true to his own purpose and guiding you to the natural ways."

"Yes, he sure is. By the way, I love the idea that the keeper of feelings is called the *Weeping Willow*."

"Yes, indeed we are truly the roots of emotion."

Jane stretched out on her side, anticipating the willow's story. "I would love to hear your lesson."

"Of course, my dear. I would enjoy the telling of it. It could be said there are as many legends about the Willow Tree as there are willow trees. Some stories cast the willow in the role of mourner, grieving for lost loves and loved ones passed. For instance, one such tale speaks of a man and woman whose love for each other was so great they would not be kept apart, even by their families' long-standing feud.

"They met by chance, along some well-used path, and fell instantly in love. But alas, each family's hatred for the other blinded them to the happiness of the couple. Time passed and each desperate attempt to gain the blessing to wed was rejected.

"Finally the star-crossed couple decided to run away. The route of their escape crossed a powerful river, and the little boat that carried them was old. Just before they reached the other side the boat hit an unseen rock and capsized, and the young woman was sucked beneath the surface of the water. Her lover dove into the icy water over and over, hoping to rescue her, but alas, the girl was lost forever.

"Every day of his life from that moment on, the husband-to-be went to the river's edge to look for her. Every day he stretched his long arms down into the water with the hope that he would find her. The last day of his long life found him again at the water's edge, searching still and hoping once again. He passed from this world in that very spot. His body became a huge willow tree; his arms became long supple branches, reaching into the water, forever searching for his lost love."

Jane felt her stomach clench. She knew the yearning one felt when something treasured was irretrievably lost. It left a hole in your heart that you never stopped trying to fill. The ache in her body subsided as Grandmother Willow went on.

"Another story speaks to the emotion of joy. It tells of a man who loved to fish. Every spare minute he had was spent by the river. Sometimes when he knew the fish would be biting, he would leave his fields and ignore his chores in hopes of catching the big one.

"Whenever his good wife looked for him, she knew exactly where to find him. He would be down at the river, fishing. And so when the man died, his wife buried him in the spot he loved most—along the river's edge. From his grave grew a great willow tree, the branches leaning over the water like so many fishing poles, luring the fish closer. Even in death, his love of fishing lived on, and so did the joy of catching the last big one."

In her mind's eye, Jane could see the old fisherman, happily baiting hooks. Nothing she had done lately could conjure the joy emanating from the man's face as he cast another line.

"Psalm 137 in the book you call the Bible tells of the Jews' capture and removal from Zion. So great was their sorrow, they could no longer bear to sing and so they hung their harps in the trees by the river Babylon. The weight of those harps pulled the branches down, forever a sign of their unhappiness. Those trees became the first willows.

"Still another tale tells a different origin of the willow. It tells of the time when Creator first placed the Willow on Earth. The little tree was so happy to be alive, and so full of the joy and wonder of living, she refused to stay where Creator planted her. She wished to experience everything life had to offer, see all the beauty the Earth held, so she dashed about madly experiencing and feeling one thing after another.

"This frustrated the Creator. Every time He looked for the little willow, she was someplace else. Her moving at will did not fit into His plan for trees, and so one day, while she was dashing from one spot to the next, He pulled her up by her wandering roots and planted her upside down. Today the long tendrils you see are actually the legs of the Willow, bending once again towards the earth in hopes of righting herself."

Jane smiled, enthralled with each story the willow related.

"I believe I could tell you a willow story for every emotion you can name because it is the Willow's purpose to remind you of the great gift of your emotions. Many of you believe that your emotions are merely a by-product of being human. I will tell you they are given to you for a reason—just as everything else on Earth has reason and purpose and lives within the divine blueprint.

"Your positive emotions, the ones that make you feel good, are a signal to you that you are living and working in a way that best serves you. When you feel negative or bad emotions, it is also a signal, letting you know that you are out of alignment with your true nature and what is best for you. Your emotions are precious internal guides you may check in with and heed.

"On this Earth, Creator left many signs—reminders and lessons for you if you have the eyes to see them. This is the great blueprint of Nature. The Willow is the guardian of our emotions and a reminder to listen to your feelings. The truest wisdom and the highest actions do not spring from the mind but are born in the heart."

Jane pushed herself into the sitting position once again. She let the words of Grandmother Willow sink in. *The truest wisdom and the highest actions do not spring from the mind but are born in the heart.* She quickly cataloged a number of emotions and took careful note of how they made her feel.

Joy, happiness, security, love, hope, trust, and peace all made her feel exactly as they sounded—happy, peaceful, right, and good. Next, she did the same with the more negative emotions: hate, anger, jealousy, resentment, guilt, and shame. Jane could have predicted how she would feel, but once again she allowed the emotion of each word to wash over her. They made her feel sad and small; even her body felt heavy and weak.

"Wow, it's true, even calling emotions to mind has an impact on my body. As powerful as some of these feelings are, it's a wonder we don't pay closer attention and realize they are signals. So, in other words, when I am making a decision I should weigh both sides of a choice and see which one gives me the best feeling. And if I choose that route will it always be in my best interest?"

Grandmother Willow's branches rustled as she answered. "Not exactly, Jane. You must understand that all things are connected. Emotions are just part of the whole. You must also use your discernment, education, wisdom, and experience to guide you. All these elements play a part in the decisions you make and the paths you choose.

"At the edge of a tall cliff, you may feel at the moment that flying would bring you the most joy, but your discernment will tell you that you don't have wings, and your wisdom will tell you this is not a good idea, and your education will tell you that in this case, gravity is not your friend."

Jane laughed out loud. Grandma Willow had a sense of humor. "So if another person makes you feel negative emotions, what then?"

"Others may try to make you feel things to further their own agendas or to gain control over you. You must remember it is your choice whether or not to accept another's intention for you. If you allow them to goad you into feeling what they wish, then you give up your power. No one on Earth can make you feel anything or cause you to do something you don't agree with. It's all your choice and it depends on what you wish your life to be and what you wish to experience."

"What if I cause myself to experience a negative emotion, like guilt or shame?"

"Guilt and shame are signals telling you that you are doing things or acting in a way that is not a part of who you really are. They are messages that contain the lesson, *don't do this again.* But most humans don't take the lesson and leave it there. They dwell in the emotion, and in time they come to believe they are somehow bad people. Over time they allow these emotions to predict for them how the rest of their lives will be. This belief that they are fundamentally bad will play out in their actions and ultimately become their destinies. The lesson of guilt is simply: *don't do that again, it isn't in your nature.*"

"What about fear?" Jane asked. She felt like she was pressing Grandmother Willow, but she really wanted to understand and be completely clear.

"Fear is an emotion that serves a great purpose in your life. It belongs only to the ego and the physical body, and has nothing to do with the spirit. The ego is charged with the task of keeping you alive. Fear is the emotion that tells you not to jump off a bridge or walk in front of an oncoming train. In this way it serves you.

"The real problem with fear is when the ego grows so strong it begins to perceive everything as an attack or a danger. That can be anything from people who are different from you, or an off-hand remark someone makes, to taking on a new experience. Fear is a powerful thing, and if you let it take control it can stop you from doing anything. Remember, Jane, there are only two ways to live and learn. One is from love, which is open and allowing; the other way is from fear, which is limiting and can hobble you."

Jane put her hand to her head and fingered the little scab on her forehead. If she had let fear have its way, she wouldn't have gone back to the overlook to see if her encounter with Grandmother Spider was real. She would have missed Max and all she was experiencing. She might have lived out her life fearing she was insane, waiting for the moment she went totally around the bend. Jane vowed at that instant she would live and learn from love.

Max interrupted her thoughts. "Jane, we should start back. We're losing the light, and although I can find my way back in the dark, you may need some light."

Dear Max, Jane thought. *Through all his disappointments he still works out of love. He knows his purpose and how he wants to express it, and because of it, he not only serves himself but me also.* Jane smiled. *I want to be just like Max. My hero is a dog.*

"Okay, Max," Jane said as she stood up and brushed off her backside. "Grandmother Willow, I can't thank you enough for all you have shown me today. I hope we can come back and visit with you again."

"It would be delightful," Grandmother said. "I know some of your kind think the flora and the fauna of this world live and die without ever noticing the human struggle, but I will tell you, we not only notice you, we are more interested in you than you will ever know. After all, we are all the same one thing. Your fate will be ours also."

Max said his good-bye and started back on the trail. Jane waved and followed along behind. *There is truly more to this world than we are ever aware of…Incredible,* she mused as she kept her eye on Max's bushy tail bouncing along in the twilight.

ELEVEN

...this is one of those moments that define your life, when all you thought you knew was just a shadow of what really is

Jane awoke the next morning to find that the rain had moved on, leaving the day brilliant and sunny. The hands on her alarm clock read nine-fifteen. She had slept later than usual. Her first impulse was to jump out of bed and get her day going, but the bed was warm and cozy and the pillow cradled her head so perfectly she decided to linger, treasuring the moment.

Max was still sprawled beside her bed, his feet moving in little jerks, with huffy little whispery barks coming from his throat as he dreamed of running in some perfect meadow. *This is heaven,* Jane thought. *This is the place I would choose over almost anywhere in the world. I wish I could stay here forever.* Deep from within the back of her mind, she heard her own voice reply, *"Then stay here."*

Jane sat straight up in bed. "OH MY GOSH!"

Her sudden outcry brought Max instantly to his feet. Scanning the room, his head bobbed over the bed and then disappeared beneath it, searching for the source of Jane's abrupt reaction.

"What is it?" Max cried. "What happened?"

"Nothing…Well, nothing physical. I was just lying here, enjoying the quiet, and a thought popped into my head. I was thinking how wonderful it would be to stay here, not go back to Atlanta, rent this place…live here. And I heard this voice in the back of my head say, *then stay here.*"

"And…"

"I never entertained the idea of moving here. This was always going to be an extended vacation, a solace, so I could get my head together. When the idea popped into my mind, I realized that I'm really free to make any choice I want."

"So it's finally sinking in, is it?"

"Yeah—it is. I mean, you always know you're an adult and free to choose whatever you want, but you never understand how much you limit yourself. I was going back to Atlanta because I thought I had to. I was going back because my life, such as it is, was there. Actually my life is wherever I happen to be at any given moment, and the possibilities are endless."

Max smiled up at Jane. "And the dawn breaks."

"No, Max, I'm serious. The whole choice thing…You get it, but you really never get it completely. It's the idea that any moment you can totally change the direction of your life. And you know what? Now that the idea of staying has rooted itself, I kinda like it. I may have to give this some careful consideration."

Jane leaned over and threw her arms around Max's neck. They sat quietly together, allowing time to stop. Jane thought to herself, *this is one of those moments that define your life, when all you thought you knew was just a shadow of what really is.*

It was Max shifting from one foot to the other that brought Jane out of her musing and back to the present. She chuckled as she realized what all the shifting meant. "You have to go outside, don't you?"

"Yup" was his one-word reply as he headed for the kitchen at a trot.

During her shower Jane flirted with what *staying here* meant. Finding a job was number-one on her list, but then again, if she went back to Atlanta she still had to find a job, so she was on level ground on that point. Housing was the next hurdle. She wondered if she could make some sort of arrangements to stay in the cabin. The real estate sign in the front yard indicated the intention to sell, but the market was so poor right now, the owners might be willing to rent it to her until the economy took an upturn.

She had no car payments—her parents had gifted her with a new car when she graduated from college—but there was the matter of insurance. Living in Atlanta caused her insurance to be rather high, and Jane wondered what sort of reduction she could get if she lived here. Then there was food; she liked food, not to mention heat and electricity. She would lose the water bill, though, because the cabin had its own well.

Wrapped in a towel, Jane dug through her purse for her checkbook and her last savings account statement. She had seven hundred fifty-three dollars and eighty-five cents in her checking account, and a glance at her statement yielded twenty-five hundred in savings. Life in the city was expensive, and without a job she would be in financial trouble in two months. Here, the cost of living was lower so she just might be able to squeak by a little longer.

The idea of staying gained ground in Jane's mind as she dressed and dried her hair. With it, the seed of hope and guarded excitement began to sprout. She grabbed her legal pad and a pen on her way to the kitchen, pausing as she passed the living room to imagine fresh paint and new furniture. She was already moving in. With Max back inside and coffee in hand, Jane sat at the kitchen table and began to sketch out the details of staying here.

"Jane—are you writing?" Max asked excitedly.

"No, Max, more like listing. Before I get too carried away about staying, I have to look at the financial end to make sure it's even possible."

"Oh, it's possible," Max said casually. "Anything you dream is possible or you wouldn't dream about it. Be careful you don't let the details of the dream kill it before you get started."

"I don't understand, Max—I thought paying attention to the details of life, like your feelings and knowing exactly what you want, is the whole point."

"It is, Jane, but it's not the same thing. Knowing what you want is vital, but how a plan will unfold you can't know or predict. You may develop an idea of how something might happen, but that doesn't mean it will happen that way. In fact, a really airtight plan can sometimes cause you to fail."

Jane put down her pen and studied Max. "Okay, confused."

"I'm saying it's better if you *intend* to stay here, not plan it out… Just *intend* it. If you make a detailed plan, set in concrete, then the first time things don't go according to your script, you can get very disappointed and quit. Intending to stay is putting your signals out to the universe and leaving open how your desire succeeds. Then when the opportunities begin to present themselves, you won't dismiss them because they didn't follow your expectations."

Jane closed one eye and gave her head a shake. She was more confused than ever. Max moved closer to Jane and went on. "Jane, you're living proof of this. You planned to come here because you wanted to change your life. You didn't like the direction it was heading. But your expectations were that in the solitude, God would speak and answer all your questions. You were listening for a thunderous voice, looking for a burning bush, hoping for an angel. Your meeting with Grandmother Spider was ordained. The visit to the overlook was no accident, yet you were so focused on getting your answers in a certain way, you had to be stopped and hit over the head to receive them."

Jane's hand went to the fading bruise on her forehead. "You're telling me I didn't have to fall, that I could have, no, *would have* met Grandmother Spider without the accident?"

"Yes, that's what I'm telling you. There isn't one single route to accomplishment; there are many ways a thing can come to pass. If you're too locked into one certain way, you can miss all the other ways, and sometimes it's infinitely easier to ignore all the other possibilities.

"This is the part you humans always mix up. You pray to Creator to move your life in a certain direction and then you go ahead and decide *for Him* what you will accept in the way of an answer. If the plan doesn't unfold just like you think it should, then you're angry your prayers weren't answered. You need to realize *how* something will come about isn't up to you; it's up to *Him* so just stay open to what shows up. The whole reason you prayed in the first place was because you *didn't know* how to proceed. You should stop telling Creator how to do His job and stop limiting Him. And while you're at it, stop limiting yourself."

Jane rolled her eyes in frustration. "So what you're saying is I shouldn't plan anything, I should just wish a certain thing will happen and it will? When I go to bed tonight I can wish for a million dollars, and tomorrow morning a bag of gold will be on the front porch."

"No, wishing alone won't do it." Max shook his head, irritated with her sarcasm. "We've been over this…just like your emotions work with your discernment, education and wisdom. It's not one thing separated from your life, it's how all of it works together. Intending is setting your mind and thoughts to a task, and then putting some action behind it. Start walking towards the goal."

"But that requires a plan, doesn't it? Some sort of plan of action?"

Max sighed. "Jane, I am not saying you shouldn't take a look at the path—call it a plan if you wish. I'm saying to understand that there is always more than one path to your destination. Don't set yourself up for failure by insisting on just one route. If one way doesn't work, get creative and find a new path."

The light went on in Jane's eyes. "Ah…I see. There's more than one way to skin a cat."

Max smiled widely. "Yes…but don't let the cats hear you say that. Look, Jane, all I'm saying is just because you don't know how your goal can be accomplished, don't give up. Take the first step and see what doors open; the next step may be very different than you thought it would be and may lead you to your solution faster than you planned. Give Creator a chance to move in your life. Life is not all up to you and it's not all up to Creator; you're co-creating this together—that's the deal."

Jane looked down at the scratching on her pad. Max's words caught hold in her mind. She felt like she had been sleepwalking her way through life. Her vision of living was so limited, narrowly focused on her perspective, when really there was so much more to it than she ever knew.

"Okay, well then…The first step is to see if I have enough money to support me while I look for a job." After five minutes of pencil pushing and mumbling, Jane tossed the pencil on the table. "I can do this, Max—I can support the expenses while I make my way through the rest of it."

"Great. What's the next step?"

"Well, I suppose I should call the landlords and see if they will even consider letting me rent the house long-term."

"Good. Where's your cell phone?" Max asked.

Jane went into the bedroom and retrieved her phone. Back at the kitchen table she hesitated before she dialed. "Max, they could easily say no. The house is for sale, not rent, and they might prefer to leave things as they are."

"If they say no, then you buy a newspaper and find someplace else to rent."

"What if I'm not able to find a job? The money I have will run out in a couple of months and then I would have to break the lease."

"Stop with the *what ifs*!" Max shouted. "The *what ifs* are just a case of the *hows* in disguise. Before you've taken the first step you're tempted to defeat yourself—this is exactly what I'm talking about. You've finished the game before you've even made a play. You don't accomplish anything all at once, you accomplish it by taking the first step and then the second and third. You're looking down the road way too far and already deciding you're gonna fail."

Jane gulped and looked at the phone again. She slowly stood up and took her jacket from the hook by the door. "I have to go out in the backyard. I'm nervous about this and I need some room to pace."

Max followed as far as the screen porch and allowed Jane to make the call in privacy. He watched her pace back and forth as she spoke. The conversation was marked by long periods of silence and then animated gesturing. Forty-five minutes later Jane shut the cell phone and turned towards the house.

"They said YES!" she shouted as she ran to the screen door. Her face was alive with excitement. Max jumped to his feet, tail wagging so furiously it contorted his whole body.

"They said yes, Max!" She went on, the words tumbling out of her mouth so fast he could hardly make sense of them. "And get this. The rent will only be four hundred and fifty a month. I can use the furniture until I can buy my own and—this is the best part—they said if I decided I really like it, they would give me an option to buy. My back rent would count as part of the down payment. Do you realize what this means, Max? We could own this place. We could have our own home!"

Max stopped in mid-wiggle and looked at Jane. The expression on his face was one of complete surprise. "What do you mean—we?"

Jane registered the shock on Max's face and dropped to one knee in front of him. "I've been thinking about this for a while. Even before I decided to stay here, I knew I wanted you to stay with me permanently. In the short time you've been with me, I have grown to love you dearly. So much so, I can't imagine you leaving after this adventure is over. It would break my heart. I know you've been disappointed in the past, and hurt, but even if this doesn't work out here, no matter where I go, I would never leave you behind. I couldn't. I am making a promise right up front: even if we had to go back to my parents' farm for a while, I would never abandon you. Please say you'll stay with me, Max."

Max looked directly into Jane's eyes, then at the cabin and around the yard before fixing on Jane again. She hadn't realized she was holding her breath until he spoke.

"It's true that my life and my companions have disappointed me in the past. It's very hurtful to be passed over or cast aside, but the past belongs to the past. I can't go back and change the decisions of those I've loved, and dragging that baggage around with me now will only keep that pain alive. I have grown to love you too, Jane, and I'd like nothing better than to be your companion and your friend. I would love to be home with you...So yes, I'll stay."

Jane hugged Max's neck so hard it nearly choked him. The two spent the next few hours wrestling and playing, cementing this new phase of their relationship. They walked around the cabin, and Max listened while Jane talked about the flowers she would plant and the ways she would change the exterior. Jane listened while Max told her his wishes for his own outside house and how he would occupy his time while she was at work.

The discussion continued over lunch, and it was decided the afternoon would be spent in town. Jane would grab a local paper and begin her job hunt. Max would come along, and the first money spent on their new home would be to purchase a dog house for him at the farm supply store. On their way back, they would stop and visit Jacob, delivering the goodies Jane had baked the day before.

The little house that once felt temporary and foreign to each was now filled with a new spirit. In the space of a few hours, it had become permanent and familiar. Max and Jane were home. They belonged somewhere and to each other, and for now, that was more than enough. Even though there was little money and the future was a big question mark, they felt like they had struck it rich.

TWELVE

*...worrying about the mistakes you might make in
the future is the same as seeking failure*

By late afternoon Jane and Max had managed to work off the
excess energy that the morning's excitement brought. Armed with a
large container of baked goodies for Jacob, they headed into town.
The first stop they made was the feed store. The two spent the better
part of an hour in the lot examining five different models of dog
houses on display. The two smallest ones were eliminated right away;
neither would accommodate Max's size. Of the three left, one had a
shed roof, another looked exactly like an igloo, and the third sported
a peaked roof with enough overhang on the front for Max to lie with
his head outside and still stay dry on rainy days.

Jane sat on a pile of bags containing potting soil and watched as
Max went in and out of each house over and over again. He checked
to see if he could turn around and stand up, and how much room he
had when he lay down. He walked around the back of each, stared at
the sides and gave them all a thorough sniff. Jane smiled to herself.
His first house had been picked out for him. This house represented

his choice, and Jane could tell he was happy with the opportunity to have a say in the matter. She wouldn't rush him. He didn't even look up when a salesman appeared from the side door.

"Well, it looks like we're shoppin' for dog houses," the man said.

Jane looked up at the large figure approaching her. The gray beard he sported hinted that he was past middle age, but his skin and eyes said not by much. He wore a flannel shirt and bib overalls with tan leather work gloves stuck in the rear pocket. His accent revealed to Jane that he was native to the area and had probably lived here all his life.

His easy manner told her he would become more than just the man who worked at the Feed and Seed. He would become a neighbor, someone you knew by his first name. When you saw him from time to time, you would ask about his wife and kids, and he would wonder how things were with you. Jane may never have dinner at his house or be familiar with the intricate details of his life, but he would become a symbol of home, an anchor holding her in the community and a familiar face that told her she belonged here.

We pass so many people on the streets of a city and never know their names or what their lives are like, but here, she would know the people she passed, like Jacob, Cookie and so many more she'd yet to meet. They would all greet her or throw their hand up when they passed her on the road. Over time they would all be woven somewhere into the fabric of her life, part of the texture and color.

"Name's Dub," the man said as he extended a large hand. "Looks like your dog's gonna have some say in the matter of his house."

Jane reached out and let his calloused hand shake hers. "Jane, Jane Morgan. Yes, Max has a mind of his own."

"They all do. My wife and I have two. Got 'em for her when the kids left home. Short of buyin' 'em booster seats so they can sit up to the dinner table, she has 'em so spoilt, ten pounds of salt wouldn't save' em."

Jane laughed at Dub's description of his wife's fondness for their dogs. She was amused by his colloquial description and because if the truth were known, Dub was probably as guilty as his wife in the spoiling department.

"You new in town?" Dub asked.

"Yes, I came up from Atlanta for a visit and like it so much I decided to stay," Jane answered as she watched Max pace back and forth.

"Atlanta. You couldn't melt me down, pour me in a gun and shoot me into Atlanta. It's too busy and there's too many people for my taste. I've been all around the world when I was in the service; there's some pretty places, no doubt, but none like this. This is God's country."

"I'm beginning to understand that," Jane said. She wondered if he had any idea how true his statement was.

"Well, I can't help with the decidin', but when it comes to the buyin', I'll be right inside. Just come on in when you're ready," Dub said as he disappeared back inside the store.

When Jane turned her attention back to Max, he was sitting in front of her. "Well, which one do you like?"

"I like the one with the overhang. Which one do you like?"

Jane drew herself up and tried to imitate Dub's voice. "It's your house. I can't help with the decidin', I can only help with the buyin'. If that's the one you like, then that's the one we'll get."

Max thumped his tail on the ground. He was as excited as a child on Christmas morning. Jane reached down and ruffled his head. "Let's go pay for it and see about having it delivered. I'm sure it won't fit in the car."

The two gave no thought to whether Max was allowed in the store; his following her inside seemed as natural as could be. He followed her past the aisles of garden tools and fishing rods, stopping behind her when the bird feeders caught her eye. With winter coming Jane knew the birds would be hard pressed to find food, and a bird feeder seemed like the perfect second purchase. When they finally made it to the counter, Jane's arms were full of feeder and bird seed. Dub was behind the counter waiting for her.

"Looks like a good day for the critters at your house."

"Yeah, Mother Nature has taken on new meaning to me lately." Jane winked at Max. "Can I have the dog house delivered?"

"Sure can," Dub replied. "Where's your place?"

Jane had to think a moment about the directions. It was the first time she ever had to give them out. "If you're headed south on Route 76, it's right off the road on the left. You pass Sky Mountain Road and it's the very next house."

"Well neighbor, I live down off Sky Mountain myself. I'll load it in the back of my truck at quitting time and drop it off on my way home. Save you the delivery charge." Dub gave her a sly grin.

When all was said and done, Jane left the store having purchased a dog house, a bird feeder, various kinds of seed, a pair of work gloves exactly like the ones Dub had in his pocket, a hammer, some nails, two bales of straw-bedding for Max's new house, a can of brown stain, and a brush to apply it with. Dub was a great salesman.

Jane shook her head as she made her way through the parking lot with Max at her heels. Life in these mountain towns was clannish; they took care of their own. She had only become a permanent resident this morning and already she was receiving the local preference as opposed to the tourist treatment. Things were definitely looking up, and she took it as a sign that staying was the right decision. She only hoped getting a job was as easy. This was a small town and jobs might not be as plentiful. She and Max had to have money coming in to make a go of it here, and until she was gainfully employed, she couldn't relax.

Max broke into her thoughts. "Where are we going next?"

"I figured we would go by Mountain Vittles and get a newspaper. We can deliver Jacob's goodies to him while we're there; it's pretty close to the time he shows up."

"You're worried about something, aren't you?" Max asked.

"What makes you say that?"

"You forget who you're dealing with. Dogs are very tuned to body language, and the big crease in the middle of your forehead is a dead giveaway."

Jane glanced quickly at Max. "I'll remember that and yes, I'll feel a whole lot better when the employment problem is solved. Then we can really celebrate."

"Worry is just a waste of energy. It's useless, and most of the time the things you worry about never happen. You would do yourself a huge favor if you stopped worrying altogether and looked for opportunities to solve your problems. If you concentrate on all the doors that are closing, you won't have the presence to notice the ones that are opening."

"I know, Max, I agree with you, but this whole trip began because of the failures in my life. My job, Dan, all of it failed. Deciding to stay here has given me new hope, and the last thing I want to do now is fail again. I mean, what says I'm not making the same bad decisions in a different location? It makes one afraid to be too optimistic."

Max stared at Jane for a moment. "Why is it so much easier for humans to believe the worst about themselves instead of the best? Worse yet, why allow negativity to be the guiding emotion for the future? You people spend so much time looking backwards, it's no wonder you can't see where you're going. No wonder you're always off the scent."

Max huffed and stuck his head out the window, his nose into the wind. Jane knew he was frustrated with her. She had been given this incredible chance to see proof that life was more designed by actions and attitudes than left to chance, and yet she was having a hard time applying the wisdom she was receiving. One minute she was good with it, and the next she fell right back into her old patterns.

Jane knew this way of being would take a bit of practice. She silently vowed that she would start to keep herself more aware of her thoughts. As for now, she wouldn't speak to Max until they got to Mountain Vittles; she would just be quiet and let him enjoy a snoot full of smells.

True to her promise, Jane drove silently the rest of the way to the restaurant. She didn't speak when she let Max out of the car or when she retrieved Jacob's box of goodies. As she and Max made their way down the park pathway, she pretended interest in the scenery and Max pretended interest in the scents. Jane's shoulders relaxed when she caught sight of the old man sitting in his usual spot. Perhaps a third person would break the awkward hush between them.

She anticipated Max's rush to greet Jacob and was shocked when he remained by her side. His enthusiastic tail was the only sign that he knew the man on the bench. As Jacob watched them approach, a broad smile creased his face.

"Well then, Max, I am happy for you! I see you have found yourself a home at last…And a good one, I suspect." Jacob took Max's head in both hands and scratched behind his ears. "Sometimes life falls together in just the right way."

Jane's mouth dropped open as she took a seat beside the elder.

"How did you know Max will be staying with me?"

"The way he walks with you," Jacob replied. "He shows where his heart is—his focus is on you." Jane glanced at Max, who was feigning disinterest in the remark. He was still annoyed with her.

"Is that for me?" the old man said as he pointed to the plastic container.

"Yes—sweets, just what you ordered. Max and I baked them yesterday. I hope you like chocolate chip cookies and brownies."

"My favorites," Jacob smiled as he took the box from Jane. "I'll have to be careful and just eat one a day; I have sugar, you know."

Jane's eyes widened. "I wish you would have told me you were diabetic, Jacob. I could have used artificial sweetener instead of sugar."

Before Jacob could answer, Max broke his silence. "Oh good, now she'll worry she's making you sick." He looked at the old man. "Jane is worrying about failure. She's decided to stay here and afraid she won't find a job, so we're taking a guilt trip through all the poor decisions she has ever made. And if that isn't bad enough, she's using those memories to try to predict her future. I don't seem to have the words to help her understand that worrying about the mistakes she might make in the future is the same as seeking failure."

Jacob crossed his hands over the treats in his lap, shut his eyes and lowered his head. Jane recognized the posture from their first visit and suspected he was searching for a story to illustrate the error of her ways. Her suspicions were confirmed when Max lay down and shot her a sly smile. She narrowed her eyes at the dog but sat in respectful silence waiting for Jacob to begin.

"Long ago among one of the great tribes of the south lived a wise man who was chief of his village. By his good fortune, this chief had two sons—twins. As was the custom and culture of his people, when the boys were old enough, he began to teach them all the skills they would need to know to become good providers and great leaders.

"The chief taught them how to track and hunt game, how to make strong snares and how to fish. He taught them how to read the weather, how to flint the best arrowheads and how to move as quiet as a whisper through the woods.

"One of the boys was very good at mastering the arts his father taught him. He learned quickly. He was strong and sure of himself and never made mistakes. The other son was not quite as strong as his brother, and while he was given the spirit to try, he made many mistakes before he mastered a task.

"Several years passed until one day the old chief had to make the choice as to which son would succeed him and join the council meetings. He knew he could choose only one of them to lead his tribe when he was no longer able, and the choice must be the wisest he could make, as the welfare of his people depended on it.

"The strongest of his sons looked forward to his father's choice with great anticipation. He just knew he would be the one to follow in his father's footsteps. In truth, the second son also felt his brother would be chosen over him, so it came as a great surprise when the chief chose the son who made the most mistakes.

"So bewildered was the strongest son that he came to his father's lodge that night to challenge his decision. 'Father,' he said, 'why have you not chosen me to follow you as chief? I am the strongest and the one who mastered each skill you taught us on my first try. My brother struggled much and made many mistakes before he mastered anything.'

"The wise old man looked at his son for a moment and then spoke. 'Yes, you were always the first; you never made mistakes. It is true your brother struggled with his lessons—he tried and failed over and over—but do you not agree, in the end, he has mastered each as well as you?' The young man had to agree that his brother was as accomplished as he.

"The chief went on: 'I can teach you all I know about hunting and fishing. I can teach you how to knap flint and make weapons that fly straight and true, but the one thing I cannot teach you is wisdom. A man grows wise with experience and from the mistakes he makes. He learns persistence and determination from his failures. Even though you were always first to master a skill, I am afraid you were never gifted with the wisdom of your mistakes.' And so it was that the second son, the one who was forced to learn what didn't work as well as what did, succeeded the chief."

Jacob opened his eyes and raised his head. "You see, Jane, it is not really our successes that determine our character; it's how we respond to our failures and mistakes that measures a person. All people know as much about failure as they do about success. For it is in the mistakes that wisdom is born. One who has never made a mistake will never know the fortitude it takes to really gain success. In your life it will never really matter how many times you stumble and fall, but rather how many times you get back up and try again. Grace and wisdom are often born on your knees."

Jane felt the heat of humility flush her face. In his own gentle way, Jacob had admonished her for worrying. She hung her head and spoke in a somber tone. "So what you're telling me is mistakes and failures aren't such a bad thing."

"That's right," the old man smiled. "It is often our pride that makes us think mistakes are shameful. It is not necessary to always be right. A mistake isn't a mistake, it's a learning process. They aren't the point at which you give up; they are the point at which you try again. There is no shame in learning."

"No, I suppose there isn't, but those lessons are sometimes tough to take. I'm breaking new personal ground here; I don't want to repeat the same pattern."

"The trick is to know a mistake for what it is—a chance to see what *doesn't* work and find what *will* work. Learn from your mistakes but don't repeat them. If one way doesn't work, try another. How many times do you think the great man who harnessed electricity got his pants shocked off before he figured out how to do it?"

"I suppose quite a few times."

"I am willing to bet he tried thousands of times before he got it right. If he had quit after his first failure, you and I would still be living by candlelight."

Jane looked out over the park. "Jacob, once again you have managed to educate me with a beautiful story—thank you. I guess I have to thank you too, Max, even though you ratted me out." Jane smiled at the dog lying at her feet.

"There is one more thing, Jane," Jacob said. "You must not speak failure either. Do not use words like *I'll try* or *I can't*. Trying something is not doing something, it is only ever trying. Speak your success. Say *I will* or *I am*. Words are very powerful; they have substance and live lives of their own. Once spoken they guide the path in front of you."

"You mean if I say I can't, then I won't be able to?"

"Yes. Your mind has given you the spark of an idea, the dream. It doesn't label it possible or impossible. It is you who judges the dream and you who labels it with your words. If you say you'll try, then you send yourself the message that success isn't important. If you say you can't, then you never will."

Jane's mind worked as she recalled the events of the day. "Wow, just today alone, I guess I've said a hundred negative things. If I am predicting my future with my words, things are looking grim! But I still don't understand how a word can impact your actions. It seems like you should be able to say anything until you act, and it's the action that predicts how your life will go."

"Actions are very important, but you can act boldly or feebly and that's determined by what you think is possible and how you speak the dream into reality." Jacob turned his attention to Max.

"Little Brother, you must take our sister here to learn about words."

Max sat up suddenly and looked Jacob straight in the eye. "I've thought about it, but you know the danger involved. I don't trust them."

"It isn't them you need to trust, Max; you know this. We only trust another as far as we trust ourselves to handle the outcome of another's choices. Can you handle any outcome? Can you protect her?"

Max shifted his gaze to Jane, his eyes softening. "I can. There are certain precautions that can be put into place. Still, you know how quick and unpredictable they are."

"Yes, I do. They live from fear, and fear robs us all of the ability to think things through. With them it is always action first and thought later. Find an old one, Max—perhaps there will be more experience in him. The young ones are too quick to strike out."

Jane listened to the conversation. She didn't like the talk of danger, but her curiosity got the best of her. "What are you two talking about? Who's dangerous?"

"Jacob feels you would benefit from the teaching on the power of words. I agree, it is very important, but it is also dangerous to deal with those who carry the wisdom. In order to hear it, we will have to visit one from the Snake Society."

"Oh…ewww…I don't care for snakes, Max. I mean, I'm not terrified of them, but I don't care for them. I think it's the no arms or legs thing. They give me the creeps, but if you guys think I need to hear this, then I can do it. Heck, a person can do anything for an hour or so."

Jane realized she was trying to convince herself as well as Max. The idea of sitting in the presence of a snake made her more than just a bit uneasy, but she was determined to make the most of the experience, and if that included a snake, then so be it.

Max inched a bit closer to her. "We aren't talking about your garden-variety black snake, Jane; we're talking about the Rattlesnake Clan. They are the keepers of their story. They are poisonous and fearful of almost everything and everyone…Doesn't make for a great combination."

Jane felt the thrill of her own fear; she hadn't counted on poisonous. Still, she trusted Max and Jacob. "I can do this, Max. I asked for this journey, remember? It came by way of grace and I don't want to stop or miss any bit of it. Besides, you said there were precautions we could take. I am willing to see it through."

Max searched her face with his eyes and found the courage he was looking for. His simple reply sealed their fate. "Okay then, we will go…Maybe tomorrow."

THIRTEEN

...words, once spoken, bring ideas into the world.
They can change what is and foreshadow what will be.

By noon the next day, Jane found herself once again marching into the woods. This wasn't as carefree an outing as the ones that came before. There was no light chatter or laughter. Max had gone out for several hours earlier in the morning and found an older member of the Snake Society that would speak with her. Now he was giving her instructions on how to handle the visit.

"We have agreed on a meeting place. I don't want to be too far into the woods, just in case," he told her. "You did bring your cell phone as I asked?"

"Yes, I have it. Now who's speaking negativity?"

"It's not negativity, Jane, it's precaution. I am using what I know about the Snake Society to make this as safe as possible. Precaution isn't negative, it's just smart. You don't go to the grocery store without a list, do you?"

"Yeah, sometimes I do."

"And when you don't have a list, do you forget things?"

"If I have a lot of things to buy, I usually forget something."

"Well, I don't want to forget anything on this trip," Max stated. "We are to meet in a clearing. There is a log on one side where you can sit, and the Great Snake will be several feet away from you. The distance between you should be out of his striking range, though he is very big and powerful. Move slowly; avoid any sudden action at all costs. Sit as still as you can till he finishes his story, and then we will back up as we leave. Try not to be scared—he can sense it—and when you speak to him, speak as softly and calmly as you can."

"Okay, move slowly, don't make sudden moves, sit still, talk softly...I've got it." Jane didn't know if she could hide her fear as well as she wished, but Max would be there and she knew he wouldn't let anything happen to her. "Are you scared, Max?"

"Not scared, just cautious. Dogs—all animals really, and plants too for that matter—don't feel fear exactly like humans do. I mean, we feel it, we just don't expect it. A human will create a state of fear in anticipation of a situation, sometimes days before. An animal or plant doesn't. We feel it in the moment we sense we're in danger. A dog, deer, possum, or raccoon will view a four-lane highway the same way he does any other piece of land, as something to be crossed. We don't fear it until the moment the headlights are on us."

Max turned his head in her direction and gave her a wry smile. "Some of us make it across the road, and some of us don't. I have felt fear and it isn't a pleasant emotion. Still, I would rather it come to me in the moment it's needed than live with it for days. Fear is only useful in the moment. Otherwise I suspect it's a torturous thing to live with."

Jane didn't reply; she got the message. Max was telling her that worry was an aspect of fear painted a lighter shade. To worry about something ahead of time was to allow fear to ruin each moment of the

144

present. Yesterday she had almost ruined the excitement of shopping for Max's new house and a lovely visit with Jacob by worrying about something that hadn't happened yet. *New rule,* Jane thought: *I won't spend any more time worrying about the things I can't control. The ones I can control, I will make the best choice I can and act on it. The others I won't worry about until I see their headlights!*

They walked for almost fifteen minutes before the woods gave way to a clearing. It struck her as strange that one's awareness could be so focused on the immediate area around one's home with not much thought given to what might be going on just a few yards away. Life was crawling, slithering, flying, and walking just outside one's personal space, and for the most part humans seemed oblivious. The idea they were meeting a rattlesnake not too far from the cabin she slept in gave her the creeps.

Jane tried to stifle her growing anxiety by changing the subject. "When Dub delivered your house yesterday, he sat it at the end of the drive. When we get back we'll have to decide where you want it and move it. It needs to be stained so the wood doesn't rot. We can do that after it's moved—or before—whatever. I want to put my bird feeder up too." She realized that she was chattering to comfort herself with thoughts of returning to the cabin, reassuring herself that everything would be fine. Shortly after this meeting, life would be safe and normal again.

Max didn't answer. His full concentration was on the far side of the clearing. When he slowed his pace, Jane followed suit. "This is it," he said quietly. "There's the log you'll be sitting on." Max stopped and so did Jane. She watched as his ears swiveled from side to side like small radar dishes. On high alert, he sniffed the air in all directions. "He's here."

Jane spoke in a whisper, "I don't see anything. How do you

know?"

"Take a deep breath and tell me if you smell anything."

Jane breathed in deeply. "Not much, just earth and the faint scent of cucumbers."

"That's what snakes smell like—cucumbers. Sometimes watermelon, depending on the type of snake. Let's go over to the log."

Jane took small measured steps forward, wondering what made a snake smell like a vegetable or fruit, when she heard it—a ticking sound like a dried gourd being shaken very quickly. Max froze and so did she. Although she'd never heard the sound before, she knew it was the warning bell of the Great Snake. She glanced down at Max and followed his gaze. It took her a minute to separate undergrowth and soil from snake, but there he was, not three feet from her.

He was coiled in a loose ring, wrapped around and around in layers so deep and folded over on another, she couldn't count how many loops there were. Max was right—he was big. Jane stared open-mouthed. Never in her wildest dreams had she imagined she would be this close to a poisonous snake on purpose. Her healthy respect for snakes was something that kept her from the woods in the spring and summer and yet, here she was, face to face with her fear. *If I can do this,* she thought, *I can surely stand up to anything daily life can throw at me.* The task of finding a job didn't seem nearly as daunting as it had yesterday.

From where Jane stood she could see the snake's markings clearly. Truly beautiful, the unique diamond pattern was unmistakable. It was so distinct and yet blended perfectly with the surrounding flora. If she hadn't been warned he was there, she might have easily stumbled over him. There was such stillness to him. He lay so motionless it was as if he were a fallen branch or patch of stones, incapable of movement.

Jane was still wide-eyed and open-mouthed when Max greeted the snake. "Thank you for coming. The human will sit over here on the log if that's okay with you?"

The triangular head came into focus as the snake raised it a bit. His tongue darted in and out, tasting the air. "Yesss, that's fine, as long as it comes no closer," he hissed. He adjusted his position to face Jane squarely, and a long ripple of rearrangement ran through his body. "I must confess to some curiosity. I have never seen a human up close. Odd-looking things, aren't they? And yet capable of such remarkable balance standing on just two legs. Is it male or female?"

"She's a female," Max replied. "Go ahead and sit down, Jane." Max began to back slowly towards the log and she copied his movements carefully, judging her distance out of one eye while keeping the other on the snake. She didn't think she could take her eyes off him completely; she was transfixed, almost hypnotized.

When Max had first mentioned "log," Jane thought of a great old tree, broad and comfortable. This log was hardly more than a perch, and she had to balance her weight delicately. She glanced over at Max who sat just to her left, head erect and ears straight up. She could see tension written all over him, and it wasn't caused by his accommodations. He was on high alert, his movements calculated and rigid.

"We appreciate your willingness to meet us. I know this is a great effort on your part. Jane is here to listen to the story of your kind and the lesson of words." It was clear Max would take the lead in this exchange, and Jane was happy to have him do it. Her stomach was tied in one very large knot.

"Ah…yesss. Very well then." The great snake looked from side to side as if he were about to reveal some well-guarded secret. There was no small talk or friendly banter, and Jane supposed the snake was as uneasy as she and Max. He would tell his story but no more than that, and both parties would hope to never meet again.

"Long ago when the world first began, the Snake Society was very great indeed, much like the human beings of the Earth. We visited with one another, ate together, traveled together, and laughed together. We lived together in villages, spoke together in councils and served each other with our various talents."

Jane could see the snake's head more clearly now. He held it above his body in an attitude that spoke of pride for his kind. The triangular shape looked like a large arrowhead. Goosebumps rose on both Jane's arms and legs. The similarity to an arrow wasn't lost on her: both were swift and, when true to their target, potentially deadly.

"We were all very much individuals, just like you humans. Our personalities and talents were as varied as our appearances. There were brown snakes and long snakes, black snakes and snakes that swam, tiny snakes and green snakes and snakes that lived in trees. Still, each was admired and welcomed for the gifts they brought to the community. Life was good for the Snake Society then. But as the seasons teach us, change comes to all things and so it was with us.

"As with any society that lives closely together, misunderstandings will occur. Noticing and accepting there are differences and diversity can sometimes lead to jealousy or envy. Such was true with the great Snake Society when we began to notice the outward differences of our brothers and sisters and forgot about the inner similarities.

"The snakes whose skins bore intricate patterns began to think they were better and more beautiful than the snakes whose skins were plain. Those that could swim thought themselves superior to those who could not.

"It was not long before our society divided into clans and accepted only those who were exactly like themselves. The copper snakes would not speak to the diamond snakes, and the green snakes would not share dens with the black snakes. The knowledge that they were still all the same one thing faded from their minds, and the idea that their outside markings were more important than their inside sameness blinded them.

"As it always is when one's awareness becomes focused on an idea, the snake clans' perception began to spread. They began to notice and become fearful of the differences of all things around them. Some creatures walked on four legs, while others walked on two. Some flew, while others lived beneath the waters. Some had feathers, others fur, still others had hard shells, while some were covered with soft bare skin. At last diversity was too much for the snake people to handle. Difference became a thing to be feared.

"The more we took notice of the world of differences, the further apart we grew from each other and the world around us. No longer did we live together in the same way we had before. And the further apart we grew, the more we gossiped about one another. The more we talked about one another, the uglier our world became until one day our hatred of diversity became so intense it overtook our very beings. It changed who we were physically, and our mouths were filled with the poison we spoke.

"Our hearts changed towards our own kind. Our belief in the oneness of all things slipped away and was lost in the belief that difference was something to fear. Our villages vanished, our society disbanded, and our fearful words brought our hatred into reality.

"Today we snakes live solitary and lonesome lives. We have chosen to become hidden and reclusive. Our fear of others is so great, we welcome no one; and our once-warm greetings have become a bite full of poison. We used our words to speak our fate. We spoke poison and became poisonous. Life for us was forever changed."

The great snake fell silent, and Jane waited for Max to speak. When he didn't, she swallowed hard and began, softly and slowly, just as Max had instructed her. "First, let me say thank you for the opportunity to hear your story. I never imagined that words could be so important—that they are, well, things that shape our lives."

The snake slowly moved his head in agreement as he spoke. "The words you speak are like windows to your beliefs. Your beliefs, the things you think, the ideas you have, all have the potential to become your reality. Words, once spoken, bring those ideas into the world. They can change what is and foreshadow what will be."

Jane gazed at the leaves beneath her feet. She was lost in the comprehension that language or ideas—abstract things—could be made concrete physical objects. Yet her logic told her that anything ever invented had begun with a thought, a belief that something was possible, and when spoken and acted on eventually became a reality. People watched birds and dreamed of flying, and those dreams became the airplane.

The snake interrupted her contemplation. "Human, understand this. We forgot who we were and where we came from. Our elders warned us many times of the power of the spoken word, and we did not heed their warning. We chose not to. Your society is in the same danger as ours once was. You speak without thinking; you criticize your own kind without care or remorse. You even sometimes speak of yourselves as worthless or unworthy. These were our fears once upon a time; they are becoming yours. You have lost sight of your potential as a species and forgotten your own beginnings."

"What do you mean?" Jane asked.

The snake unwound a few loops of his long body and slithered a bit closer to her and Max. It was as if he wished to make sure his next words were clearly understood. Jane could feel his intensity as he spoke.

"How did life begin here on the Mother of us all?"

Jane's mind scrambled for an answer. "Well, there's a lot of conflict around the subject, what with the Big Bang theory and evolution, but for me, I guess I would have to say Creator began life here." She was beginning to become more uncomfortable than she already was. The Great Snake's proximity to her was unnerving and her mind was blank. She wasn't at all sure she knew what answer he was looking for.

He hissed back quickly, "Yesss, but how did He create it?"

"I...I don't know...I'm not sure how He created it..." Jane stumbled over her words.

The snake's head rose higher, his eyes meeting hers directly. "He spoke it—He spoke life into creation."

Although Jane wasn't much of a church person, she did try to read the Bible once, and now her mind brought up the words of the first page instantly. *Then God said, "Let there be light" and there was light... Then God said, "Let the waters under the heavens be gathered together in one place and let dry land appear" and it was so...Then God said, "Let the earth bring forth grass," and so it was.*

"OH, my God." The revelation hit Jane full force.

"Yesss...Now you see it, don't you? Now you ssseee," the Great Snake said. "Life didn't begin with a written contract or from a much-labored blueprint. It began in the breath of a spoken word. Never forget the power of the spoken word, human, for your breath will carry your words into creation."

Jane's head spun. Every time she spoke in a negative way, she was on the road to creating a negative situation. Every time she spoke of another person in jealousy or judgment, she was separating herself from her fellow man. She remembered the times she said *I can't,* and then she couldn't. Had she created her own failures? Was she really limiting what was possible for her with the words she spoke? Jane knew for sure she had created distance and destroyed friendships with nothing more than mere words. *Could it be I destroy or create my own life with the same language?*

"What you have told me will change the way I speak forever. I never imagined—" She never got to finish her sentence. Jane had been so wrapped in the story and conversation, she didn't notice the squirrel on the tree behind her and she hadn't noticed Max catch his breath. She hadn't seen Max's eyes grow wide as the squirrel jumped from several feet above into a pile of leaves below, and Jane was unprepared for the crashing sound that came after. Already tense, Jane startled and fell backwards off the log.

It all happened so quickly and yet it seemed like slow motion. Her eyes fixed on the Great Snake as she fell, watching his instant reaction. The constriction of all the muscles in the once-languid body happened in a split second. Everything was in motion. There was a blur of golden fur blocking her from the strike, and the sound of Max's painful yelp. In less time than it took to draw a breath, it was over.

FOURTEEN

...lose your power and you're powerless to help someone else

Jane struggled to right herself, clamoring back over the log. Her eyes probed the area for any sign of the snake. A slight stir in the bushes captured her focus, and she caught a glimpse of the heavily buttoned rattle sliding quickly into the undergrowth. Jane could hear her heartbeat, a rapid staccato pounding against her eardrums as she scanned the landscape for Max. She found him lying still as a stone, just off to her right.

Jane scrambled on her hands and knees through the dead leaves carpeting the forest floor. Tiny brambles grabbed at the skin on her hands, but she didn't feel it. Panic had overridden her senses and separated body from mind. She had only one objective—to get to Max. He was only five feet from her, but shock robbed her of coordination. She skittered and crabbed her way along like the heroine of a movie scrambling down a long dark hallway that grew inexplicably longer with each step. Her limbs would not cooperate with one another, and crawling suddenly became a herculean effort. The once friendly car-coat she wore was now her enemy, wrapping around her legs, catching beneath her knees and restricting her movements.

"Max! Max!" she screamed through a throat constricted around her fear. *Please...please be alive! If you're alive, there's a chance,* her mind shrieked. Only when she scooted past his bushy tail did she notice his flanks moving up and down—proof of life. Dragging herself the length of his body she cradled his shaggy head in her hands. Max's brown eyes were open and locked on hers.

"Max, oh my God. It'll be okay, Max; it'll be okay, I promise. Did he bite you? Where did he bite you? You'll be alright—I'll get you out of here. Don't worry. I'll get you to the vet."

Max interrupted Jane's hysterical diatribe. "Calm down, Jane. Breathe." Jane tried to take a deep breath but only managed a few ragged gasps. She clutched for what little control she could muster before he spoke again.

"First, are you okay, Jane? He didn't strike twice, did he?"

Jane lowered her forehead to his. It was almost too much to bear knowing that his first concern was for her. "Oh my God, Max, don't worry about me! I'm fine. He's gone. Where did he bite you, Max?"

"My leg," he grimaced as he tried to move the injured limb.

Jane raised her head and saw Max's front leg as he held it bent at the knee and slightly off the ground. She moved herself into position to get a better look. She saw it then. A dark purplish knot about the size of a golf ball had already formed. Near one edge of the swelling were two small droplets of blood. It looked like some sinister red-eyed version of a smiley face...without the smile.

Jane covered her face with her hands. "This is all my fault...all my fault. If I hadn't been so insistent...If we'd never come here, this never would have happened!"

"Shhh, Jane," Max whispered. "This isn't your fault; I made the decision to bring you here knowing all too well what the danger was. I knew what he was before we started this morning. I guess I thought I had everything covered...Didn't plan for that squirrel, though." Max gave a shallow snort and twisted his head towards her. "Damn squirrels—nothing but tree cats."

Jane heard a panicked giggle escape her lips. "Now is not the time for your cat humor. I have to get you out of here."

"I can probably walk; I just had the wind knocked out of me. He was a big one. I anticipated the bite, but I'm glad I was in the air when he hit me; otherwise he might have broken my leg...I feel like I've been hit by a freight train."

"You can't walk, Max—that will only spread the poison faster. Just lie still and let me think," Jane said as she fought to list her options. Grabbing the cell phone from the pocket of her coat she flipped it open. No service. She scanned the area looking for anything that might present a solution. No luck. *I can't carry him; he must weigh at least seventy pounds. There are lots of downed limbs; maybe I could make a travois with two of them and my coat. No, that won't work—with nothing to secure the coat to the branches it would fall apart on the first effort.* Shock was replaced with a sense of urgency, and whatever survival instinct she had was focused with laser sharpness on Max.

Jane searched her memory for the knowledge her dad had given her about the woods and survival. She wished she had listened more intently, but at that time in her life, her idea of a good campfire was one located in the lobby of a luxury hotel. The one thing her dad had stressed was never to go into the woods without a knife and a pack of matches. With those two items, you could survive just about anything. *Great, I'm not spending the night. What was it I read about not cutting a snake bite or trying to suck out the poison? Doesn't matter, I don't have a knife. What about snake bites…think, Jane, think.* She had to get Max to a vet. *What did Dad say about snakes?*

Her mind raced to open rusty memory-files. She was slashing through information on fishing, camping, fire building, canoeing, hiking…HIKING…there it was. *Rattlesnakes warn you with their rattle, copperheads are silent strikers. Rattlesnake venom is deadlier than copperhead venom; you have two hours.*

Two hours…how much time has passed? Jane glanced at her wrist and damned her new habit of not wearing her watch; she could only estimate the time. *Ten, maybe fifteen minutes have passed. I have an hour and forty-five minutes to get Max to the vet. We walked maybe fifteen to twenty minutes into the woods; how long will it take to get him out? Half hour, forty-five minutes if I'm lucky. How long?*

Jane ran the time-table over in her head only a few more seconds before she sprang into action. The one thing she knew for sure was that thinking wasn't doing, and she wouldn't get Max to the vet squatting there. The faster she got him to the antidote, the better his chances. If she went over the two-hour mark, there would be little hope.

The thought of losing Max sent an electric bolt of terror through her body that flung her into motion. If she couldn't carry him, she would drag him. Jane ripped off her car-coat. It was all she had, but it might work if she could slip it under Max and drag him. It was slightly longer than a jacket and she might be able to get most of his body on it.

Jane went behind the dog and rolled one side of the coat in on itself, pushing it as far under Max as she could manage. Sliding around him, she gently rolled him over on his back and pulled the bunched coat under him, spreading it out as she went.

"Max, can you wriggle up and lay your head in the hood of my coat?"

"Yes, I think I can," Max answered, using his shoulders and hips to inch along.

Jane helped the process as much as she dared. When he was situated where she wanted him, she zipped up the coat and pulled the drawstring at the hem as tightly as the bulky material would allow. It wasn't as tight as she would have liked—his body could still slide down, but his hips wouldn't get through the opening. He wouldn't fall out. Time wouldn't allow for do-overs. She would use the arms of the coat as handles and drag him back to the cabin.

Once everything was in position, Jane grabbed the arms of the coat and gently raised them as high as she could without Max sliding to the bottom. There was no hope of standing in an upright position; it looked like she would be crouching most of the way and that meant slow going. *How much time had passed? Another twenty minutes... That leaves just an hour and twenty-five minutes.*

"Okay, Max, here we go. This might not be so comfortable, but it's all we have," Jane said as she dug her heels in and started to pull. "You okay?"

There was no answer from the folds of the coat. She loosened her grip from the sleeve and looked at Max's face. His eyes were half lidded; his jaw hung open, his pink tongue lolling out the corner of his mouth.

"Max, answer me, stay with me! Max, stay with me...MAX!" Jane screamed. There was no response. She could see he was breathing, but the rhythm of his breath had changed. It was becoming slower, shallower, with a ragged edge to it. The poison was beginning to make its lethal trek through his system.

Terror clutched Jane's chest. She repositioned herself and held her breath against the effort of her initial pull. It worked—they were moving. Walking backwards, stooped and straining under Max's weight, she could only manage little shuffling steps, but they were moving. The carpet of fallen leaves allowed the synthetic material of her coat to slide easily. *Thank God it's fall. At least there is some insulation from the rocks and debris that would ordinarily snag the coat.*

Every five or six steps Jane would slow to look behind her, charting her path in small increments. From this tree to that rock, from this rock to that bush, she worked her way back towards the cabin, retracing the route Max had forged only a short time ago. Every few minutes she would stop, straighten her back and catch her breath. She looked for landmarks that would tell her she was still heading in the right direction. Getting lost was out of the question. Max didn't have the time.

Time...how much time is going by? Jane thought. *Hurry...Hurry... Hurry.* The word urged her forward. She was afraid to check on Max's condition, afraid of what she might find. The snake was huge, and Jane couldn't begin to guess how much venom a snake of his size could make or how much he had injected into Max, let alone how rapidly it now moved in his body. *What if I'm wrong, what if we don't have two hours?* was the recurring thought she fought to banish.

Fear and fatigue sapped her stamina. Pulling was becoming increasingly difficult as the muscles in her back and legs screamed for relief. *How much further...how much time do we have left?* was the mantra driving her forward. The fifteen-minute walk into the woods might as well have been a two-day hike. Despite help from the fallen leaves, the bottom of the coat snagged on protruding twigs and larger stones, inhibiting her progress. Tufts of down were strewn on the path behind her like the breadcrumb trail from some fiendish fairy tale. The small goals she achieved helped to bolster her resolve: *from this tree to that bush, from this bush to that rock.* She was making progress. This time when she turned to check her route, she saw a break in the tree line. Her backyard was only a short distance away—her backyard, her car and Max's salvation.

When Jane broke free from the tree line, the coat slid easily through the short grass. After pulling Max to the edge of the gravel driveway, she ran to the cabin to get her car keys. She stole a quick look at the clock on the kitchen wall. *How much time?* Racing back outside, Jane gently eased Max over the crushed stone to the back of the SUV. *I just need to get him into the car. Once I get him into the car, everything will be okay.*

"We're almost there, Max...We're out of the woods, we've made it to the car...almost there, boy...Hang on," Jane babbled as she opened the tailgate. There was no reply.

Taking a deep breath, she slipped her arms under the coat. Cradling Max's limp form, she pushed up with her legs. His body was almost even with the back of the car when his weight began to shift inside the coat. The slippery material that had once been her savior was now the enemy. There was too much room inside the coat and too much coat to get a solid grip. Off balance, Jane dropped quickly to the ground. Her already tender forehead hit the bumper, and sharp-edged stones bit into the back of her hands and dug into her knees.

"Shit...shit...shit!" she cursed loudly. On all fours and close to collapsing, she hung her head. *So this is how it will end. Here in the driveway. Figuring out how to get him out of the woods and the long painful crawl back to the cabin was for nothing. You're too weak to lift him into the car. Max isn't here to think for you, and you can't do this alone.*

A small whine made its way from Jane's chest up to her throat and became a keen as it escaped her mouth. The sound tore away what was left of her strength and she rolled on her back. It went on and on until she had no oxygen left and she found herself sucking in great gulps of air. The voice in her head hammered on. *That's right, just lie here and hyperventilate—hasn't it always been this way? You're powerless alone. Haven't you always just been a player in someone else's life, a side-kick to someone else's dreams? That's why you cling to Dan, isn't it? Because without him, who would you be? You lose yourself in other people's lives because you can't build your own.*

All this talk about choice and potential is very nice, but when it comes to putting it into practice, you just can't cut it...and the lessons just get bigger, don't they? Lose your power and you're powerless to help someone else. This time it isn't just you losing...this time it's Max...

"SHUT-UP!" Jane felt something inside her break loose. She forced herself to count each inhale and exhale until she was under control, and all the while little bubbles of anger floated up inside her. Pulling herself into the crouching position, she began to rip the coat away from Max.

"I will not fail—I'm not that person anymore. I can do this. Max isn't going to die and I'm not giving up!" Jane shouted. Her fingers, numb with cold and stiff from exertion, refused to obey her commands. Mustering every remaining ounce of patience, she fumbled with the zipper and strings.

"I will do this...I will win."

At last the coat fell away and she could see Max lying there. The swelling had spread, creeping up his shoulder. Jane stared intently at his flank—he was still breathing. Once again, she slid her arms underneath him as she summoned all her strength.

"God, give me the strength. Just help me get him in this car." The muscles in her legs shrieked with pain. The cry moved up her body and broke from her lips in a primal groan. Pure adrenaline drove her body up to the rim of the bumper and she hoisted Max into the back of the SUV.

The next few minutes passed as a dream. She was aware of the keys in the ignition, the SUV in reverse, the roar of the engine as it sprang forward, but it was as if someone else were driving. Jane watched from a far-off place as her deadened hands manipulated the steering wheel. Time was once again having its way with her. She sped past Mountain Vittles in what seemed only a second, and yet the road in front of her stretched out in an unending ribbon.

Jane's heart leapt when the Feed and Seed came into view. In her mind's eye she could see Dub inside, smiling and chatting with a customer, both unaware of the life-and-death race passing on the road outside.

The little green information sign snapped her back to the present. The vet's office was only two blocks away from the hospital—just one right turn and she was there. Her foot pressed the brake just enough to make the corner safely. Thankfully there had been no traffic on the main road, but now Jane was bearing down on the car creeping along in front of her. *No time...I have no time for this.*

The little white head gave no sign that it heard the horn blasting behind it. To Jane it looked as if a giant Q-tip was driving the vehicle, and yet for all its exaggerated size, it could barely be seen over the dashboard. Once again, her body took control and she automatically swung into the other lane, speeding past the elderly obstacle. Her car screeched into the parking lot of the vet's office. Flinging the door open, she was out of the car and through the door in seconds.

"Would somebody help me, please!" she shouted as she entered. "My dog has been bitten by a rattlesnake and I need help carrying him."

Time stood still in that moment. The doctor's office became

a tableau. The receptionist froze, pen in hand. Two veterinary assistants stopped in their tracks and stared open-mouthed at Jane. Waiting-room dogs took a break from their nervous pacing and stood immobile. A cat in a crate sat motionless and wide-eyed, and the bustling sounds of the busy office gave way to silence.

Jane found the eyes of a male assistant. "MOVE!" she screamed. "NOW!"

FIFTEEN

...sometimes life just happens

In an instant the young man found his feet and sprinted behind Jane to the back of the car. He scooped Max up in his arms and rushed back into the clinic. They were through the swinging gate of the reception area and into an examination room in less than a minute. No sooner had the door shut behind them when a second assistant and the vet appeared through another door.

"Hi, my name is Doctor Slater," the vet introduced himself, already bent over Max.

"Jane Morgan."

"You said your dog was bitten by a—"

Jane didn't let him finish his sentence. "Rattlesnake."

"How long ago did this—"

"Less than two hours, but longer than one." Jane anticipated the doctor's questions and answered before the words left his mouth. "It was a really big snake. He needs the anti-venom now."

The doctor continued his exam as Jane impatiently watched. He listened to Max's heart through the stethoscope. "Let's get an IV started," he said to the assistant. Removing the ear pieces, Dr. Slater ran his hands over the dog, stopping here and there to probe more deeply, paying special attention to the snake bite. Jane's patience hit its limit. She knew the anti-venom was crucial to Max's recovery, and he needed it now.

"Would you please just give him the antidote?" Jane ordered tersely.

"We don't usually give anti-venom. We don't keep any in stock. It has a short shelf-life and it's terribly expensive. Snake bite is rarer than you think, and we can't afford to buy it just to have it expire. We treat the symptoms like swelling with steroids and run fluids to flush the toxin from the dog's body. Then we—"

"You don't have any anti-venom?" Jane interrupted.

"Let me finish," the doctor said in a compassionate tone. "This being the tourist area it is and with the Appalachian Trail running through our backyard, the hospital in town does carry a supply of anti-venom. It's been some time since the bite, there is considerable swelling, and your dog is lethargic and unresponsive. I think you're right—since we can lay our hands on the antidote, it would be wise to use it. I just want to warn you it isn't cheap."

"I don't care about the cost," Jane retorted. "Just get it for him!" She watched as the assistant shaved a patch on one of Max's legs in preparation for the IV.

"Okay, Sam, call the pharmacist over at the hospital and tell him you are on your way to borrow a vial of rattlesnake anti-venom." Sam picked up the phone in the examination room and dialed. Jane half-listened to this conversation while she watched the vet carefully thread the IV needle into Max's vein. "We have a dog that was bitten…anti-venom…okay, good…at the main entrance desk…yes, I will be right there...thanks" was all Jane heard.

Jane searched the walls of the little room and found the clock. *Time, are we in time?* Stepping to the head of the table, she wound her fingers into the thick fur just behind Max's ears. Slowly she began to scratch him. He liked to be scratched behind the ears almost as much as he liked having his belly rubbed. She looked up in time to see the doctor staring at her hands. Jane hadn't noticed until now, but the backs of her hands were badly skinned, with little pinpoints of blood dotting their surface.

"So, how did this happen? It's pretty unusual to see a snake bite at this time of year. It's too cold for them to be out for any length of time. We tend to see snake bites in July and August."

"We were hiking in the woods," Jane began. She was getting pretty good at lying to doctors, so the rest of the story flowed along nicely. "We were about fifteen minutes into the walk when Max got struck. I guess the leaves crunching under our feet hid the sound of the rattle. He just came out of nowhere."

"You look a bit banged-up too. Your hands took a beating, and you have a bump on your forehead."

"I guess it must have happened while I was trying to lift him into my car. He's heavier than he looks. I almost dropped him."

Dr. Slater continued to try to make conversation. Jane knew he was attempting to calm her, but she found no comfort in the small talk. She kept her eyes on the clock, watching the little hand click off the seconds.

"Are you cold, Miss Morgan?"

"What?"

"I asked if you were cold." The doctor looked up at her. "You're not wearing a coat."

"I used my coat to drag Max out of the woods."

Reaching over the counter, the vet pushed a button on the wall. Within seconds the receptionist poked her head in the door. "Get Miss Morgan a cup of coffee and see if we can find a blanket for her."

Jane wasn't interested in coffee or a blanket, but all the talk about her physical condition was bringing her back into her body. "Come to think of it, I am kinda cold." With that admission, she began to shiver violently. The events of the day were beginning to take their toll on Jane. She hooked the plastic chair next to her with her foot and dragged it close enough to sit down. Her hands never left Max.

"How long does it take to walk to the hospital from here?" she asked through clenched teeth.

"It won't take Sam ten minutes to get there and back. It's one of the advantages of life in a small town—nothing is very far away." He changed the subject again, obviously feeling Jane's tension. "Are you a visitor to our village?"

"No, I'm new in town. I haven't been here long enough to get the lay of the land. I only knew where your office was because I passed it once on an errand." Jane was silent for a moment and then broached the question that both she and the doctor had been avoiding since she arrived. "Is Max gonna make it? Is he going to live?"

Dr. Slater stopped what he was doing and looked into Jane's eyes. "It usually takes about twenty-four hours to know for sure. There have been cases where a dog was unresponsive to treatment, but with the anti-venom and the IV, if he makes it the first twelve hours, he should have a pretty good chance."

Jane laid her head against Max. All the panic, fear and struggle up to now had just been a prelude to hurry up and wait. A heavy feeling sank into her bones. She would live hour to hour for the next twelve hours and then another twelve just for good measure before she could know if Max would be okay. *This is beyond cruel,* she thought.

Where is that damn guy with the medicine?

No sooner than the thought popped into her head, Sam came through the door carrying a small brown bag. Jane watched as the doctor drew the liquid from the tiny vial and injected it into the IV. Though it was colorless, she could see it swirling and mixing in the bag. Jane scrutinized the drip-chamber, watching each tiny drop as the anti-venom moved slowly into Max. Sighing deeply, she laid her head back on the dog and silently willed him a message. *There it is, baby, you have the antidote. This is all we can do for you...the rest is up to you.*

Jane opened her eyes to see Dr. Slater's trouser legs in front of her. He had a couple of adhesive bandages and some kind of swabs. "Let's have a look at those hands."

Jane reluctantly let go of Max and held them up. The doctor ran the swab over the backs of them and secured the bandage strips. Turning them over, he examined her palms. "All good here—how about that forehead?"

Again with the forehead, Jane thought. It was sore and there was a slight nagging ache, but she wasn't about to admit it for fear Dr. Slater would order her over to the emergency room for a quick check. She didn't want to deal with explaining yet another injury in the same spot as her last. This time they might not be so dismissive of the explanation.

"I came down on my knees pretty hard," Jane said, deflecting attention from the bump.

She rolled the legs of her jeans up as the vet crouched down to have a look. "No broken skin, but you have an ugly bruise on your left knee. It will be sore for a couple of days, but no permanent damage."

The receptionist came into the room bearing a white blanket and coffee in a styrofoam cup. Handing the coffee to Jane, she draped the blanket around her shoulders and left.

"That should make you feel better," Dr. Slater said. "You sit here and drink your coffee; I'll be back and forth to check on you. I have some other patients to see."

"Thank you," Jane replied, "and thank your receptionist too."

"No problem," he said, shutting the door behind him.

Jane swallowed the hot liquid gratefully. She could feel the first gulp make its way down to her belly. Chilled to the bone and weary, she felt the adrenaline wearing off that had bolstered her earlier in the day. Her back felt stiff and strained, and muscles in her legs that she never knew she had protested at the slightest movement. None of it mattered; it would wear off in a couple of days. All that mattered was Max.

Alone in the little room, Jane leaned in and whispered in Max's ear: "I know you can hear me. You're going to be alright...you have to be alright. It was your choice to take me on, and you're not getting out of it this easily. You're stuck with me. As far as I'm concerned, you haven't fulfilled your purpose by a long shot. So you just lie there and let the medicine do its job. I'll be right here—I'm not going anywhere...I love you, Max."

Dr. Slater, true to his word, was in and out of the room the rest of the afternoon. Assistants strolled in to change the IV bag and listen through stethoscopes. In between their visits, Jane talked to Max about the plans she had for the cabin and all the things she would like to do when he was well. She even told him fairy tales from her childhood—anything so he would hear her voice and know he wasn't alone. She was there and would be for as long as it took.

Right in the middle of Jane's telling of her particular take on Goldilocks and the Three Bears, the doctor entered the room.

"Well, look whose eyes are open," he said. "Seven hours and we're seeing improvement. I believe Max here is gonna be just fine."

Jane abruptly stood up, spilling the dregs of her coffee over the floor. Dashing around the table she saw Max with both eyes open and breathing normally. His eyes focused on her as she moved closer to his head. He drew his lips back in a weak smile, one the vet would have interpreted as happiness at seeing his master, but Jane knew it was Max's version of "gotcha."

"Max…oh thank God you're awake! You're going to be okay! I thought I'd lost you, Max. I was afraid I wouldn't get you here on time, but everything is going to be alright now." Jane stroked his head, cooing and fussing over him as the doctor checked his leg.

"Can I take him home now?" she asked.

"No, Jane, not just yet. I would like to keep him the full twenty-four hours. We'll run a few more IVs in him to make sure all the toxin is flushed from his system. If everything goes well, you can take him home tomorrow afternoon."

"You want me to leave him here overnight? I can't leave him alone. If he's staying—I'm staying."

The doctor paused for a moment, analyzing Jane's reaction. When he did speak, his tone was soft and hushed, as if he were speaking to a mad woman. "Jane, you can't stay here. You need to go home and get some rest. This afternoon has been somewhat of a trauma for you too, and now that we know Max is going to be fine, you need to take care of yourself. Now, it's almost six-thirty and we'll be closing the office soon. In just a bit I am going to have Sam carry Max outside and let him relieve himself—he's had a lot of fluids this afternoon. Then we will transfer him to a cage so he can rest. There isn't anything you can do for him here. Go home." Before Jane could protest again, he left the room.

"He's right, Jane, go home," Max said. "You haven't eaten and you're exhausted. I would be poor company for you. There isn't a thing you can do here except be uncomfortable or keep me awake, and you heard the man, I need my rest."

Jane ignored his plea for her to leave. She narrowed her eyes and hissed, "Why didn't you tell me you were awake?" She tried to sound stern, but she was so happy that he was okay, she couldn't muster any real ire.

"What, and interrupt a perfectly good story? I wanted to see if the bears stuck to their vegetarian ways or if Goldie was now on the menu," he said smiling broadly.

"Max, do you have any idea how worried I was?"

"I was going to tell you when you finished. Honestly...I hadn't been awake long and I was just enjoying the fact that you were here." Max's smiled faded and he looked at Jane soberly. "It means a lot, Jane, more than you know." Max paused, and Jane could see he was moved by her loyalty. "Now go home, rest, eat, and for Pete's sake take a shower—you're a mess."

"Alright, I'll go, but I'll be back around noon to take you home."

Jane trailed behind Sam and another female assistant as they carried Max out back. He stood for a minute, shaky on three legs, and then hopped around the enclosure looking for just the right fence post. The two aides followed behind him like parents of a toddler just learning to walk—close enough to catch him if he fell, but far enough away to allow him his space. Following them back into the office, Jane hovered as they placed Max in a cage and attached another IV bag to the outside. When they left the room she spoke to Max again.

"Okay, looks like you're all set. I hate to leave you here, Max... Are you sure you'll be okay?"

"Go, Jane...I need a nap." He glanced around the kennel. "Besides, look around—if I feel the need to be social, I have plenty of company.

Can't say I care much for this cage, though."

"Serves you right for the stunt you pulled when you woke up." Jane smiled broadly. Reaching in to stroke his head she said, "I'll be here tomorrow...I love you, Max."

The mischief left Max's eyes as he stared into Jane's. "I love you too." With that he rolled on his side and shut his eyes. "Try to keep yourself out of trouble tonight. I'll be right here when you get back."

Jane reluctantly left the kennel area and walked to reception. She discussed the paperwork with the lady at the front desk. All of it could be done tomorrow when she felt more herself. Relief at Max's recovery had taken her over. A bit of food and a good night's sleep was all she could handle at the moment.

She drove home slowly, stopping only to grab some fast food from a drive-through. As her car pulled into the driveway, the headlights rested on the empty dog house. They hadn't even had time to move it to its rightful place in the backyard. Staring at the peaked roof, she recalled how excited Max had been shopping for it. What if Max hadn't made it? What if he had died on the steel examination table? She would have come home to the dog house, sitting there alone like an unused specter of things that might have been.

Jane took a deep breath and exhaled. In that one breath she let go of what remained of today's event. She thought of how close she had come to losing Max. The physical strain and heart-pounding fear drained away, and as if her body needed to be completely washed clean of it all, the tears finally came.

How long Jane cried she couldn't tell. At first, long wracking sobs, the kind that make it hard to catch your breath, shook her small frame. Eventually they gave way to a more controlled, steady weeping ending in frequent fits and starts of sniffling and ragged little breaths. She used every napkin she had in her bagged meal, throwing them on the floorboard of the passenger side. It felt wonderfully cathartic to let go and give her emotions free rein. Rather like ending a sentence with a period, it brought closure to the horror of the day.

When she had cried herself out, Jane grabbed her food and made her way to the house. Sitting at the kitchen table, she listened to the silence. There were no clicking toenails on the hardwood floors. No quiet breathing or muffled snorts that were part and parcel of a good doggy-dream. The cabin felt empty and cold, devoid of the energy that another living soul carried.

There was a *thrum* another living thing gave off—a kind of presence that reached out and mixed with yours, as real and as tangible as a physical touch. When someone else was home with you, even if you weren't in the same room, the air took on a vibe, an electric quality that let you know you weren't alone. At the moment, her presence wasn't enough to bring any kind of warmth to the house.

Jane got up and went to the living room. She switched on the TV and let whatever show it was tuned to bring the cabin to life. Another voice, no matter whose it was, was company. Turning up the volume, she then made her way down the hall past the bathroom and into her bedroom. She would have loved a hot shower, but she knew she didn't have the energy to brush her teeth, let alone scrub her body. Ripping back the covers on the bed, Jane slipped out of her shoes and dropped her jeans and shirt in a pile on the floor. Crawling into bed, she propped the pillows slightly and drew the quilts up chest high.

Unwrapping the cold burger and fries, Jane munched slowly. The food had no taste; the magic of any kind of special sauce was lost on her. It looked good, but even her taste buds had lost their ability to function. Halfway through the meal she looked for something to wipe her hands.

Funny, she thought, *I used all the napkins as tissue in the car and now I'll have to use tissue as napkins. I never seem to do anything the way it's meant to be done. If it hadn't been for me, Max would have never been in the woods today talking with the rattlesnake, and he would have never been bitten. Then again, we both understood what could happen and we went anyway. Sometimes life just happens. The important thing is...I didn't fail him. No matter the circumstances, I got him to the vet's and he's going to be okay...I didn't fail.*

Jane smiled as she rolled on her side and grabbed a couple of tissues off the nightstand. All the muscles in her back complained. Her arms were stiff and sore, and the bruised knee wouldn't let her forget it was there. Wiping her hands clean, she tossed the wad on the floor. It could wait until tomorrow. Everything could wait—a shower, her clothes, everything. She closed her swollen eyes for a moment but when she tried, they refused to reopen. The long blink gave way to a deep sleep...and that's when the dream began.

SIXTEEN

...there was a time when man felt responsibility and great respect for the Earth and lived in the rhythm of her seasons

Jane was pinned against the ceiling looking down at her bed, watching herself sleep. She never wondered why there was two of her or how she could be in bed, deeply asleep, and bumping along the ceiling at the same time. It all seemed perfectly normal and so very pleasant, aside from the fact that the bedroom suddenly felt small and restrictive. Jane looked at the half-eaten burger on the bed and the fries migrating along the quilt with every move the sleeping Jane made. The pile of clothes was still on the floor, right where she dropped them; everything was just the same as it was when she was anchored to the floor. Her dream perspective was rather like looking into a giant dollhouse: interesting, but hardly exciting. Still, she made a note to dust the top of the mirror.

You hardly ever get to see your house from the top down, Jane thought as she checked the moldings on the two windows of her room. *This particular view would come in handy during spring cleaning.* Through the open window she could see a slice of grass and wondered how high she would float if she were outside. No sooner had the thought crossed her mind, she was propelled towards the window, through it and outside.

Jane glanced back looking for broken glass but there was none. She had simply passed through it like the breeze through the screen. Now she was above the trees, floating along peacefully, awestruck at her new-found freedom and all she was able to see.

The night was crystal clear and ink black. If it had not been for the glow of the little villages and towns dotting the landscape, the bond between heaven and earth would have been complete—no beginning, no end, and no horizon—just dark endless blackness broken only by pinpoint starlight.

Bare trees reached up at her like children, arms outstretched, grasping for some invisible mother. The cold autumn night didn't touch her; the air was merely cool and delicious against her skin. Jane felt like everything she saw belonged to her and her to it. Every sight, sound and smell passed through her as pure joy. It was freedom like she had never known, limitless and unbound by any law of nature. She swooped and floated, shot high in the sky and dove straight down again, flirting with the earth, and daring gravity to try to hold her.

Jane was just about to do another barrel-roll when she heard something—something that didn't belong to the night. Faint and distant, the music of a flute teased her ears. Haunting, almost mournful, it echoed off the mountain tops and snaked through the valleys. Straining to locate its source, Jane dangled motionless in the night sky. Scanning the horizon, her eyes caught a glow far too bright to be another town. Silvery and shimmering, it pulsated and danced in perfect rhythm with the music, beckoning her, pulling her deeper into the mountains. Mesmerized, Jane gave in to its summons and allowed herself to be drawn forward. Whatever was calling her, she would follow.

Floating along on light and sound, the tune passed through her, vibrating in her chest. It entered her body effortlessly, coiling around her heart, weaving itself into her emotions until it joined with her soul. Jane thought she would burst from the bitter-sweetness of it. Tears escaped her eyes, falling freely, as if all the sorrow and pain she had hidden away through the years were being wrung from her body. Healed by the melody and cleansed by the radiance, she wanted to stay in the moment forever. Living there, wedged between the notes and the stars, she was free of the persistent cravings of her body, unbounded and infinite. But even as she reveled in the feeling, she felt herself being slowly drawn down to the earth.

She descended gently through the forest until her feet touched down on the edge of a wood. The source of the luminous light revealed itself as a large lake that lay in the center of a meadow. The surface was still and unbroken, the meadow itself guarded on all sides by the thick forest. Standing on the shore of the lake and ringing it entirely stood the animals, one of every species and size native to the Carolina mountains. Splendid in their form and flawless in their colors and markings, they appeared to be the sum of what was perfection for their kind. Their coats glittered and gleamed, bathed in the glistening light of the lake, giving them an unworldly aura.

Jane stood perfectly still. Her eyes went from animal to animal and found each staring back at her with anticipation. Their gaze flicked back and forth between her and an enormous white bear. Even though they were in a circle with no beginning and no end, it was evident he was the leader. The air was charged with a powerful energy that sprang from the animals themselves. There was much snorting and nervous pawing of the ground. It was obvious there was purpose to this meeting and whatever it was, it was of great consequence.

The animals were lined up next to each other in perfect order. Only one gap remained—an open spot next to the white bear indicated the absence of one species. The moment her eyes fell on the gap, Jane knew the spot was where mankind once stood and where she was to stand now. She felt no fear as she walked to the edge of the lake and took her place. The ever-present music grew soft and tranquil as the white bear spoke.

"Welcome, Little Sister."

"Thank you," Jane replied, still distracted by her partners in the circle. Each was now silent and still. Stepping into her place brought perfect order, and everything was peaceful and in complete harmony. "Where am I?" she asked.

The white bear's voice rumbled deep and commanding, "You are at the Enchanted Lake. It sits at the base of the mountain your kind calls Clingman's Dome. This is the Council of Animals. We have been waiting for you."

"Why am I here?" Her voice was steady; all of this seemed perfectly natural.

"You are here because you are one of the few who have decided to know the truth of life on Earth. You have chosen to know who you are and what it means to be human. You have chosen to find your true nature, and in making this choice, you have found those that share this planet with you."

Jane stared at the bear, her eyes blinking as she fought to understand. She couldn't remember ever making a conscious choice to know herself or discover what it meant to be human. There was only the anger at not managing her life and the constant feeling there had to be more to it. "You give me too much credit," she said plainly. "I don't remember asking for any of this; I only remember being angry and confused."

"Your anger was frustration at not finding what you sought. Your discontentment was your heart telling you there was more to life than others could answer. It was your persistence that drew you to this journey. Your courage to see beyond the answers you were given and to seek the truth is what brings you to us now."

Jane looked around the circle again. Her stomach twisted into a ball as she sensed that at any moment the reason for her presence would be revealed. "I am not courageous at all. In fact, I have only begun to learn how scared I was to step into my life and fight for my dreams."

"We know, Jane, and under different circumstances we would have given you more time," the Great White Bear said, suddenly sad. Looking down into the water he went on: "But there is little time left, and so few of our two-legged brothers and sisters have made this same journey, so it was decided you should come now."

"I am very grateful for the invitation, but I still don't see why you would want me…" Before Jane could finish her statement she heard a familiar ticking. Glancing to her right, her eyes came to rest on the representative of the Great Snake Society.

White Bear snuffled, "You were about to deny your greatness for the third time, Jane. I believe you learned about the power of words just yesterday."

"Yes, I did. You would have thought the lesson would have made a lasting impression on me. All of this takes practice, a real shift in the way you see yourself and life. I won't forget again." Jane nodded at the Great Snake. "Let me just say thank you for the invitation and leave it at that."

"The invitation has always been open to your kind. But so few of you will allow yourselves to hear it or even believe it is possible. We try to reach you every day with messengers from our side of life. It may be a sparrow flying low in front of your car, the branch of a tree grabbing at your hair or the scent of flowers reaching your nose. We try to speak to you of the weather and warn you of the earthquakes, but you are blind to us. You don't see us as part of the oneness, as fellow citizens of the Earth. To most of humanity, we are resources to be used, things to be controlled and manipulated."

"I don't see you that way, not after Max and the others I have met. Is that why I am here? Do you have a lesson for me?"

"Not a lesson, Jane, a story maybe—perhaps more of a plea."

Jane said nothing. By now she was accustomed to the silence of thought. Looking around the circle she could see the others had become hushed. The air was thick and heavy, and she knew whatever was said here tonight was of the greatest importance to them all.

"This lake is called the Enchanted Lake because it does not exist to human beings, or rather it does not exist to them anymore. At one time, your kind always stood with us here, in the very spot you stand now. But the Lake has become the stuff of legends. It can no longer be seen by human eyes because we chose to hide it at the time the first man separated himself from us. Today, only a very few will ever see it. Those that can hear us or feel us will eventually find their way here, but no one else." The bear dipped his paw into the water, causing silvery ripples to spread across the surface.

"This water has the power to heal. It has always been so. Any creature that may be injured or suffers from a physical ailment comes here to bathe. A deer wounded by a hunter's bullet can swim in the water and come out whole. Even those sick in spirit can rest in the water and be renewed. This place is sacred to us, and it is where we meet to hold our most solemn councils.

"After man left us, he lost his way completely. Greed, envy and the quest for material possessions took root in his heart. Man lost his common sense, his memory of all his relatives, and the quest for material things began to drive his reason. He would have tried to own this lake and, failing that, polluted it as he has the air, the soil and the other great waters of the Earth. It was our decision at that time to close the eyes of those who sought to rule it and hide its location and its magic. That was a very sad day, Jane, a day that changed our world as we knew it.

"There was a time when man felt responsibility and great respect for the Earth and lived in the rhythm of her seasons. He knew the plants and animals as his family and honored them for their purpose and the sacrifices they made. Now, he forgets us…and the Mother. His arrogance is so great he believes he has dominion over everything and uses it as he pleases. But know this, Jane—he lies even to himself. The natural laws of the Mother just *are* and will always *be*. The more you try to change her, the more she will fight for survival. Man's greed has already caused great changes in her, and even though he is a beloved child she nourishes, she will show him no mercy. She will defend herself, changing so quickly that man will not have time to adapt and he will die away. The Mother will be left to heal and live on, but man will not be here and unfortunately we will follow you."

Jane watched as the circle stirred, uttering quiet grieving sounds. Red blotches of embarrassment spotted her cheeks. *So this is it, the reason I'm here. They know we're killing the environment and ourselves, and we're dragging them down with us.* Embarrassment turned to humiliation as she realized that until a week ago, neither the problems of the environment nor the plight of animals would have registered on her awareness scale. A week ago, it was all about her.

Now silent, White Bear watched Jane as if reading her thoughts. He waited for her to digest the meaning of what he had said. When her eyes returned to his, he went on.

181

"Many of your elders are lulled into complacency by thoughts of comfort and entitlement. You have enjoyed the abundance of the Earth without thought to replenishing its wealth. Too much is used too fast, leaving no season to renew. Your kind has built many wonderful things and also many terrible things. The by-products of your imagination are sometimes poisonous and destructive.

"You must understand that life also has its seasons, and great building can be followed by great destruction. Those things you have created, which do not work in harmony with the natural world, will fall away and be destroyed. The level of destruction and its severity will be determined by your ability to foresee the future and change before it's too late.

"What our human brothers and sisters do affects us all—so many of us have already disappeared. Species of great beauty and grace that once walked among us have faded into extinction, and it all happens so fast. Since we seem to have no voice in your world, we seek those whose voices may be heard. We see great potential in you, Jane, and this is why you're here. We brought you here to ask for your help."

Jane's eyes widened. She stood speechless, trying to grasp the magnitude of their request before asking, "What can I do?"

"Because of what you have seen and heard in your experiences among us, we hoped you would speak for us. Help your kind remember where they came from and tell them we still wait to embrace them as they come home."

Jane put her hands over her eyes. Her heart was breaking as she wondered how many of her kind would listen. Yet here among the animals, witnessing their anguish, she knew she had to do whatever she could. Standing in her spot at the Council she felt truly whole and more herself than she had in a long time. White Bear was right: with her knowledge came responsibility. She lowered her hands and sighed deeply, "Yes, of course, I will do whatever I can."

"We know not all will have the ears to listen or the eyes to see what is to come, but there are some who will, and a great many more you may be able to persuade. If you show them their power and help them find their voices, then the leaders of your Councils must surely listen. We know what we ask; we have asked it of others too. None have failed us yet, but the more humans that know, the greater the awakening. There is so little time left to change the path."

"How much time is left?" Jane asked.

"Two winters, maybe three."

White Bear's words hit Jane like a rock. The idea that in two or three years all this could be gone—the trees, birds, plants, animals, even mankind—was so overwhelming she couldn't breathe.

The animals around the lake grew restless, talking among themselves and looking at Jane with great pity. "They sense how you feel and they cry for you," White Bear said. "This is no easy thing we ask." He turned fully towards her. "Time is short, but before you go, bend down and wash your face in the lake. Bathe your eyes and fill your ears with its water. Pour it over your hands and let them soak in it; it will bless you and help you, for it is truly magic."

Jane did as she was instructed. Kneeling down, she peered into the pristine water. Fish of a hundred kinds were huddled close to shore, listening to what had been said. A wide smile spread over her face as she remembered what Max had said about the way fish felt about humans. Now they moved closer, flipping and jumping in the lake like an invitation for her to share their amazing world. Doing as White Bear instructed, she drew the water up in cupped hands, washing her face, splashing her ears and wetting her head. Holding her hands under the surface she watched as the spirit of the lake imbued them with its silvery cast. When she was done, White Bear spoke for the last time. "We honor you and your kind. For us, one more lost relative has found her way home."

Before Jane could return the compliment or even say goodbye, she felt herself being pulled back into the air. As quickly as she had come, she was returning, all the while her mind asking, *How…How will I help them…How will I help us?*

As she approached the cabin, music once again reached her ears. Not the alluring flute of the Enchanted Lake that beckoned the soul and refreshed the spirit, but something familiar and contemporary. Demanding and intrusive, it yanked her back through the window into her sleeping body.

SEVENTEEN

...I'm not afraid of you anymore, Time. You won't tick away the minutes of my life without me present.

Jane roused, fighting her way back up from the depths of sleep. She seemed to be dragging the invasive tune of her dream with her. It wasn't until she opened her eyes that she realized it was morning, and the annoying jingle she heard was the ring tone of her cell phone, blasting away from the nightstand.

She grabbed the phone blinking rapidly to focus on the caller ID. It was the vet's office. Panic rose to her throat at the thought that Max had suffered some sort of setback, but the voice on the other end of the line was calm and professional.

"Ms. Morgan, this is Natalie from Dr. Slater's office. I called to give you an update on Max. He's fine, recovering well. Dr. Slater says you can pick him up after lunch. We re-open the office at one p.m. so if you'll be here then, we can fill out all the paperwork and you can take him home."

Jane agreed and hung up. Jarred and disoriented, she lay in bed giving her heart a chance to slow to its natural rhythm. She closed her eyes again, searching for any serene remnants of her dream. It took only a moment to reconnect.

The visions from the night before stuck to her brain. Clear and vivid, the dream was as real as anything she'd ever experienced in her waking hours. It was as if she had actually been to the Enchanted Lake and spoken to White Bear. *That will teach me to eat fast food right before I go to sleep,* Jane mused. *I'll have to tell Max all about it when I get him home—he'll get a kick out it.* She pushed the vision to the back of her mind, recalling the events of the day before and how close she'd come to losing Max.

On instant replay, she thought about yesterday's nervous walk to the rendezvous point, Max stiff-legged and weary, the conversation with the Great Snake, the moment of the attack and the hell that followed. What stuck in Jane's head was the snake itself—his long body lying in a relaxed coil. Parts of his length draped over the ground as if muscle and bone weren't a part of him. The triangular head and green slanted eyes, cold and unforgiving in their gaze, would loom large in her memory.

A floorboard creaked in the hall and Jane's body convulsed, pulling in on itself and rolling her into the fetal position. "Holy mother of pearl, Jane, shake it off," she said out loud, laughing at her reaction. "It's over…get a grip." Even as she relaxed, she suspected she would be jumpy for a long while, but as Max would say, time would have its way with her and the images would fade. The only fallout would be a heightened respect for nature.

A figment of last night's dream floated past her eyes. Despite the events of yesterday, this morning she felt a greater love for nature than she ever had before. There was sacredness to the natural order of things. Even though Mother Nature could be unforgiving to those that did not speak her language or understand her laws, you couldn't argue her divinity. Jane was in love with her, awed by her. The deeper she probed nature's mysteries, the more chaotic and senseless the man-made world seemed. Nature kept her promises and Jane respected her for that. She even held a grudging respect for the Great Snake.

Pulling herself into the present, she slid out of bed slowly, giving her sore body time to readjust to movement. Limping down the hall to the kitchen, she repeated her morning routine of coffee and a shower. *Man, that dream seemed real,* she thought as she spread her arms out wide, trying to recapture the feeling of flight. *Now I know what bliss feels like.*

Jane did her best thinking in the shower. She always had. Perhaps White Bear was right; water is holy, like a baptism. Each morning you are born to a new day, a chance to begin again, correct your path, and forgive others and yourself for the mistakes of yesterday. Maybe it was no accident she felt so renewed and refreshed after a good hot shower.

Body scrubbed and hair washed, Jane stood under the hot stream a minute longer. She decided to make this part of the day a ceremony— claiming a moment to list all the things in her life she was grateful for, all the things she already had, like this cabin, food, her health, and the gift of waking to another day. She would make it a point to recall all the things that made her feel good, like ice cream and the smell of rain. She would give thanks for all that brought meaning to her life, the people she loved like her mom and dad and her beloved Max. Yes, she would even thank Dan for giving her the opportunity to understand what she didn't want in a life-partner. Taking this little bit of time each morning would remind her of all she already possessed. Starting each new day grateful and happy would help her anchor the lessons she was now practicing and keep her eyes open to the delight of unbounded possibility.

Jane towel-dried her hair, inadvertently rubbing the ever-present bump on her head. It was still sore. The shower had done nothing to relieve her mild headache. As she examined her forehead in the bathroom mirror, her mother's voice popped into her head. *This too shall pass.* She smiled; she hadn't spoken to her parents in a while. Once Max was home, she would call and fill them in on all she was doing...well, almost all. Telling them everything would most likely result in a drug interrogation or a quick visit. She wasn't ready for that.

Moving through the bedroom, she tidied up as she went. Discarding the old burger and fries brought yet another flashback from last night's dream. An image of the shining lake and White Bear's sad eyes flickered at the back of her mind. The melody of the pan flute that seduced her seemed to be just out of reach. Straining to hear it again, she found it living in her memory as a poor copy of the original.

Jane dressed, applied the blow dryer to her hair, and for the first time since she'd arrived, dabbed on a bit of makeup. Looking at her watch on the dresser, she picked it up and fastened it to her wrist. *I'm not afraid of you anymore, Time. You won't tick away the minutes of my life without me present to witness them.*

The aroma of freshly brewed coffee drew her to the kitchen. She passed through the living room, turning off the TV as she went. Coffee poured and mug in hand, Jane leaned against the counter. The house was as silent as it had been last night, but not the same kind of silent. Last night's silence was the kind that shrank you down and left you feeling invisible. It was the sort of quiet that required something or someone else to validate your existence. This morning's silence was different. It vibrated with anticipation, as if the house were waiting for her to bring it to life.

And she would. The cabin would be hers and it would be her heartbeat and her life echoing from its walls. The fear of not getting a job seemed small in contrast to the life-and-death struggle of yesterday. Even if it meant flipping burgers for a while, it would support the dream she dreamed years ago and set aside. It was the life she wished for, and she would simply find a way to support it.

Jane looked around the kitchen. It could use a fresh coat of paint—something cheerful and bright. While she was at it, she could paint the old brown cabinets too. White would perk things up. She had never allowed herself the time she deserved to discover who she was alone. Going from her parents' house to sharing a room in college, she'd then moved into Dan's apartment in Atlanta after only a brief stint in her own place. She'd been living with someone else's choices for years; it was time she had a space to express her own.

She glanced at the piece of embroidery Max had her read the first full day they were together. She would have it remounted in a nice new frame under protective glass. It would hold a prominent spot on the wall so she could see it every morning and never forget what it meant. Jane read the quote out loud: "I show you doubt to prove faith exists."

The woman who arrived here a short while ago was very different from the one standing here today. The Jane she used to be lived in doubt and fear. She doubted her choices and feared her future. She even doubted God. That Jane discounted every gift and talent she had been given and marked her success through other people's eyes. The Jane of today understood that the quickest way to become nothing was to try to be something for everyone else.

Grandmother Spider's web had shown her the threads of her life, including the crossed and tangled strands, which in their own way added to the beauty of the pattern. Disappointing and painful strings, they had become the catalyst for change. There were too many starts and stops, too many loose threads. She had allowed other people

189

to make her choices for her with an offhand remark or a bit of unsolicited advice. Constant anxiety over what someone else might think or say about her dug the hole that eventually buried everything that made her special and unique.

People could easily ignore their talents, take them for granted. A gift comes to a person so easily; it could appear as a small and insignificant talent. Because the ability comes naturally, one could forget that the task may be awesome and impossible for someone else. Lost in the perception that the talent has no value, you could lose it, let it slip past, when all the while the world was waiting for you to share it.

Strolling into the dining area, Jane could hear the deep bass of Grandfather Oak's voice. *Stop choosing complicated. If the best expression of joy and fulfillment for you is to write, then write.* Her laptop sat on the dining room table covered in dust. An ironic smile pulled at the corners of her mouth. There was her passion and her purpose waiting for her, unused and dusty. Tracing the outline of a bear on the cover, she knew it would take courage, persistence and determination to bring her talent to life. It would also demand a good deal more organization than she'd practiced in a long time. *I can do this,* she thought. *Max will need some time to recuperate, and the bedroom next to mine will make the perfect office. While he's getting his strength back I will write and keep writing.*

Jane glanced at her watch—three hours left until she could spring Max. *I haven't cleaned anything since I arrived.* Bringing him home to a tidy house would be a fresh start for both of them.

Scrounging around under the sink cabinet and the laundry room, Jane found enough cleaning supplies to get the job done. There was an ancient vacuum cleaner tucked behind some shelves where a washing machine should be, and although it was awkward and weighed a ton, it worked, and she was in business.

She scrubbed, scoured and polished her way through the cabin until every surface gleamed. Open windows allowed the crisp fall air to replace the staleness of the closed house. Humming to herself as she went, Jane mentally took stock of all the changes and repairs she would make to the cabin. All of them required money; some of them required a handyman that would also require money. It didn't matter. This morning she had no fear of the future and all things would come in time.

Jane's mind ran to Dan. *Too bad things won't work out between us. It would be nice to have someone help me with all of this, but then again, Dan isn't handy and doesn't want to be; he breaks out in a rash if he even looks at a tool. Besides, the country wouldn't suit him. He loves the hustle and bustle of city life.*

Dan's choices were not hers, she understood that now. He had a right to his choices as she had a right to hers. Her expectation that she could mold him into someone perfect for her was foolishness. Trying to force him to be what she needed only caused aggravation and resentment on both sides. Silently she vowed never to try to change the nature of anything or anyone. Never again would she trust a snake to be anything but a snake—she'd learned that the hard way.

Jane checked the time on her watch. She'd been hard at housework for just an hour and it had paid off. The house's personality shone through. Stowing away all the cleaning supplies, she grabbed the can of stain and the brush from the table and headed outside. *I can get the first coat of stain on Max's house and do the last when we're home. That way it will have a chance to air out and be ready for him when he's well.*

Squatting in the driveway, she pried the lid off with a flat stone. Three sides of the dog house had been coated when she felt something crawling up her leg. Still jumpy, she squealed and brushed away a small black ant, painting her shin brown as she did. Just her luck—she hadn't noticed a line of ants laboring over a French fry she dropped the night before.

"Ouch, that hurt," a teeny voice said.

Jane froze. She knew the voice came from the ant, but for some reason she thought it was only possible for her to hear the natural world when Max was with her. The realization that the gift of universal language was hers alone struck her like a lightning bolt. It was *her* ability not Max's that made this possible, and she might as well start owning that too.

Jane turned her attention back to the ant. "I'm…I'm sorry, you scared me."

"Well, geez, overreact much? It's not like I'm poisonous or anything. I don't even bite."

"I didn't see you. I didn't know what was crawling up my leg."

"Obviously…Now that you mention it, you're getting a bit close to our trail with those enormous feet of yours." The little black ant didn't have the same reverent tone to his voice as Grandfather Oak. Nor did he sound sweet and supportive like Grandmother Spider. This little guy spoke like he moved—quickly and to the point.

"Oh…sorry," Jane said as she checked the ground behind her for stragglers and stepped back. "I see you guys found one of my fries. Are you taking it back to your nest?"

"Yup, we have lots of hungry mouths to feed."

Jane watched as the ants marched to and from the food. Each ant carved off a bit of potato and immediately started his trek back to the hill. Her eyes followed the unbroken line of workers till she found a small mound of crumbly dirt at the far edge of the driveway. "It's remarkable how fast you can dissect something and carry it home."

"We're built for it. That's what we do; we're the clean-up crew."

Jane smiled. "The clean-up crew?"

"Yeah," the little ant went on, "Crows, buzzards, worms, ants—we clean up and recycle what you cast off or whatever has run its life cycle and passed on."

"You mean like dead animals on the side of the road?"

"Yup, soon as some animal takes the final dirt nap, we move in to recycle and repurpose what's left."

In spite of herself, Jane giggled nervously. She wasn't used to this light-hearted approach to death. "Dirt nap—that's kind of callous, don't you think?"

"Not at all. You humans think when death occurs, it's all over. That's not true. The essence of what we are never dies; the spirit lives forever. Think of the body like a shucked peanut—the shell is there, but the nut is gone." The little ant laughed at his own joke. It sounded like a tiny wind chime dancing in the breeze. "Once the spirit is done using the body, the body can still serve. Nothing happens without a reason and everything has a purpose."

"So your purpose is to deal with death?"

"No." The little ant sighed in exasperation. "I told you before, our purpose is to recycle and repurpose. Death is a term you humans invented. You see, Jane, in our beginning we chose this work; as you know by now, all things do. Nature works in perfect harmony. Everything has seasons. Spring is the time of rebirth and renewal; summer, a time of maturing and bearing fruit; the fall, the harvest of all that's been planted; and winter, the time of withdrawal and peace.

"When something reaches its winter, it cannot remain as it is. Its purpose is finished, the journey is complete. But what is left may still have another purpose, for the good of all. Creator, in his infinite wisdom, made provisions in the blueprint of life for everything, including repurposing what remains. The first ant, knowing our species would be legion, chose this intention as ours. In our recycling and repurposing we find our food—transitioning those winters back into springs and helping to keep the world clean."

A deep wrinkle marked Jane's forehead as she struggled to follow the ant's explanation. "Okay...I think I understand."

Ant sighed again, put down his chunk of French fry and leaned one spindly black arm against the morsel for support. "Look at this French fry. The potato it came from reached its winter the moment it was picked. It was no longer able to grow, and you humans repurposed what remained. You peeled it, sliced it, cooked it, and it became your nourishment. This is exactly what we do. Eventually, everything goes back to Mother Earth. Eventually everything becomes the soil from which new springs are born. We all take from Earth, but we all give back.... Great little plan, isn't it?"

"Yeah...wow...I get it now. It's part of the oneness of everything, the way it all works together, links to each other."

"Now you're gettin' it. And if you look closer, you will see how the seasons work in your life too," the little ant commented, intertwining his long feelers in front of him.

"Well, I do...get it, that is...I mean, I know I won't live forever."

"No, Jane, look deeper. Even within the journey of your life all the experiences you have also have seasons. Events, actions, decisions, relationships, even things that once served you may not now. They have seasons of their own. Sometimes a thing or person is perfect in the moment; then as you change and become more of who you are or want to be, they no longer serve. When they reach their winter, you take what remains, learn from it, use it, and move on."

"So, it's okay to change your mind and choose something else?"

"Of course," the ant replied. "You're always changing and growing. The experiences of your life force change. You're not the same person you were ten years ago; heck, you're not even the same person you were yesterday. You can always choose again. There is no limit on choices—you have as many as you wish."

"When you explain it that way, I can see it so clearly. As a matter of fact, that's why I'm here, to repurpose and recycle my life into something much finer, something that serves me better. My purpose is writing, but not the kind I used to do. So, I'm choosing to repurpose my purpose."

"Ah, writing, that's a good one," the ant said. "Expanding the possibilities and exciting the imagination—what a gift. To inspire those in humanity is a wonderful thing. Imagination is the soul's language; inspiration is the divine breath of creativity." Ant looked wistfully off, antenna twitching; an innocent smile touched his tiny face. In a moment he came back to the present and Jane. "So what will be the purpose of your purpose?"

"What do you mean?" Jane asked, scowling again.

"Just what I said, what purpose will your gift serve?"

"Gosh, I hadn't thought about that yet."

"Look deeper, Jane, always look deeper. To know your purpose and use your gifts is one thing; using them for *A Purpose* is another. The purpose of your purpose brings meaning to what you do, and that, my giant friend, is the whole enchilada. Life doesn't get much better."

Ant's description of purpose and meaning triggered the memory of the quote that had haunted Jane's days in Atlanta. *"The two greatest days of your life are the day you were born and the day you figure out why."* Images of animals standing on the shore of a lake flashed behind her eyes. Perhaps she'd already caught a glimpse of what would bring real meaning to her purpose. Her mind was floating around the edges of an idea, but before she could connect the dots the ant broke the chain of her thoughts.

"What is it you hope to give the humans that read what you write?"

Scrambling to refocus herself, Jane answered, "Let's see... inspiration, hope—to move them somehow, enlighten them in some way."

"Lovely. So you see, it's not only having purpose, it's also in the way you go about using the purpose."

"Okay, so if your purpose is to recycle and repurpose...stuff, what way do you go about it that gives your purpose...well, purpose?"

The ant turned and looked at all his hive mates working diligently at the French fry. In the time Jane and he had been talking, they had whittled it down to little more than a speck of what it once was. "LOOK DEEPER...Look at the way we carry out our purpose. That piece of potato was at least four times my length and twenty times my weight. I could have never carried it to the hive by myself, let alone gotten it down the opening."

Jane stared at the fry as the last bit was whittled away. "No, not the way it was, but when you carve it up into little pieces, it becomes possible."

"Exactly. That's the way we accomplish it, a little bit at a time. You can do anything if you break it down into small chunks and eat away at the whole. And the way we do it brings meaning to our purpose. Taking on the job of moving the French fry as it was would be overwhelming and almost impossible. Breaking it down into small parts and tackling it bit by bit makes it do-able. How we accomplish our purpose will also serve your life if you let it."

Jane shifted her cramping legs carefully. "How will it serve me?"

"Oh, come on, Jane, I know you're bright—try to keep up, for Pete's sake. When you settle on your purpose and what you wish to accomplish, sometimes the whole can look too big to achieve. The way we ants achieve our goal is to break down our task into little do-able pieces and work at it until it's completed. We're here to remind you that anything can be done by taking one step at a time."

"Yes, but you have a lot of friends helping you."

"Yeah, and so do you. When you publish a book, do you have to cut down the tree and make the paper first?"

"No."

"No, you use the talents and gifts of others. You rely on them just as we ants rely on each other. Everyone and everything serves, Jane—we're all here to help each other. None of us is totally independent or alone. Remember that. Don't ever quit on your dream. Take it one step at a time and use others' gifts and talents to forward your goals. That's the recipe for success."

A smile lit Jane's face. Until today she had seen ants as little thugs that spoiled her picnics and invaded her kitchen cabinets. But Ant had given his wisdom, making her take a deeper look at the world of helpers she had around her. It was a lesson on the connectivity of life, how each depends on another's talents to bring his own to light. Allowing others to express their gifts not only makes your accomplishments easier but brings meaning to the purpose of theirs. "Thanks so much for your explanation; I'll think about it when I tackle a project that overwhelms me. How cool—nature outsources."

"No problem. Now if you don't mind, I have work to do; there's still lots of time before dark and I can get started on something else."

Time—the word straightened Jane's spine. What time was it? Was she late to pick up Max? She whipped her watch up in front of her face. Forty-five minutes remained before she had to be at the vet's office. Enough time to clean up and, if she was quick, stop to get Max a little welcome-home gift.

EIGHTEEN

...humans think of their lives in different aspects.
That's true...they have faces and personalities for each.

The trip to town was pleasant. Jane felt like a different person. No, not a different person, she finally felt more like Jane again. Optimistic and full of excitement about the future, she drove slowly and concentrated on investigating her new hometown. As Ant stressed, she wanted to look deeper. The things she'd already missed surprised her. Housed in a big red barn was an antiques dealer. It wasn't fifty feet from the road but she had never noticed it before. She passed a stained-glass studio whose sign advertised lessons. *That would be fun. I always wanted to learn how to do stained glass; that would be a great new hobby. While I'm at it, I'll be bringing meaning to the teacher's talent. I love how this all fits together, how all the parts add to the wholeness of everything. How could I have not seen it before?*

With just twenty minutes left until the vet re-opened, Jane entered the Feed and Seed on a mission. Dub was behind the counter, as much a fixture in the place as any rack of packaged seed or barrel of dog chow. He greeted her warmly and inquired about how Max liked his new dog house. Jane had to take a minute to tell him about the snake bite, and for the next ten minutes, Dub and everyone else in the store regaled her with their snake stories. Just when she thought she might jump out of her skin, she managed to break into the conversation during a rare lull.

"Dub, I'm on my way to bring Max home now and short on time. I wanted to get a dog bed for him to recuperate on, one that you can use inside."

"Gonna baby him around a bit, are you? Well, I guess I would too if I were in your shoes. That's one lucky dog." Moving from the counter he led her to the far side of the store. "We have some nice beds right here." Halfway down the aisle, the tops of all the shelves were stacked with dog beds in every color and size.

"Some of these are a little fru-fru for my taste," he said. "This one here's a dandy. The cover is washable and it's filled with cedar so there's no doggy smell. They sell these in one of them fancy outdoor catalogs, so you know it's nice." He pulled down a Max-sized bed. It was square, firm and dark green.

"That's perfect," Jane said, eyeing her watch. "I'll take it." She kept the chit-chat to a minimum as she paid for the bed. It was almost one o'clock and she wanted to spring Max from his cage as quickly as she could. She laid the new bed in the back of the SUV; he could ride home on it if he wanted.

Pulling into the vet's office she was so excited she almost forgot to put the car in park. Natalie was behind her desk with the paperwork waiting. Jane almost fell out of her chair when she saw the total bill. Dr. Slater was right, anti-venom was expensive, but if that was the price for having Max with her, she would pay it gladly. She wrote a check for part of it and made arrangements to pay the rest off monthly. As she closed her checkbook she noticed a planter of violets sitting on the corner of the desk. Reaching out, Jane stroked one of the leaves gently. "Thirsty" was the single parched word that came from the plant.

"Natalie, your violets are dry. They could use a drink."

The young woman looked at Jane with shock and poked her finger into the pot's soil. "Oh my, they are dry! I'll give them some water just as soon as we're finished here."

A few minutes passed as Jane was given final instructions on Max, what to expect and when he would be fully recovered. Sticking them in her purse, she followed Natalie back to the kennel.

There he was, her Max, looking every bit of disgusted and antsy. The young woman opened the door to the cage and Jane threw her arms around the dog's neck. "Let's go home," he whispered in her ear.

The same assistant that carried Max in yesterday now helped Jane get him into the back of the SUV. Before he could get back into the office, Jane had the car in reverse, backed out and on the road. Alone together, they both started speaking at once. Max won the toss.

"I thought you'd never get there. I am so glad to be outta that cage."

Jane laughed. "I came at the time they told me, Max. How ya feeling?"

"I feel okay, a little unsteady…But really—really glad to see you." He babbled on in excitement. "I discovered I don't like being locked up, not fond of IVs either. Did you notice the spaniel in the cage next to mine? Well, yesterday they neutered him. I thought if I had to hear him gripe and moan about his lost sire-hood one more time I would rip through those metal bars with my teeth. At which point his lost sire-hood would've been the least of his worries. Hey, I like this bed—when did you get this?"

"On the way here, I stopped and bought it from Dub. I wanted you to have a nice soft place to rest and recuperate. It's your welcome-home present." Jane looked in the rearview mirror and saw Max smiling his doggy smile. When his eyes met hers, his expression suddenly changed dramatically.

"You've been to the Enchanted Lake, haven't you? You met the Great White Bear?"

Caught completely by surprise, Jane almost drove off the road. "How do you know about White Bear and the Enchanted Lake? I was going to tell you all about it when we got home! But I didn't actually go there, Max—it was all a dream."

"Dreams are as real as your daily life, Jane. A dream is where your spirit goes at night to help you make sense of the events of your physical life. When you sleep, you are free of the body. We all live twenty-four hours a day, Jane, not just when you're conscious to the world around you. It was no dream. You were really there, at the Council of Animals. All of nature knows about the Enchanted Lake. It's legendary. I've always wanted to be called, but you actually went. You saw them and spoke to them. They asked you for help, didn't they?"

"Whoa," Jane sputtered. "First of all, I didn't know that about dreams. Why didn't you tell me this a long time ago?"

"I did, when we spoke of angels the first day we met. Remember I told you their work is mostly done in dreams and inspirations?"

"Yes, I remember, I just didn't quite get the whole picture. Max, I flew there. It was incredible." Jane's world and the concept of what that included was expanding so rapidly she could hardly keep up. "Max, they did ask for help. If all this is true, how am I ever going to help them?"

"It will come to you."

As Max spoke, a snippet of the conversation with Ant ran through her mind. She was grasping at something that wasn't clear yet. If she just gave it some time, it would come into focus. Putting it out of her mind, she returned her attention to the dog. "Max, where did we go so wrong? How could we humans have gotten ourselves so out of tune with the universe we live in and not know it?"

"But you do know it, Jane. You're reminded every day; the news is full of talk of global warming, pollution or another animal species nearing extinction. You just think there is nothing you can do about it or wait for the government to fix it."

"I guess it feels too big. Like one person can't effect the change needed to fix such a huge problem."

"It is too big for a single person to fix, but if one person did what he or she could and then another and another and you insisted your leaders and corporations did what they could, little by little things would start to change."

"You know, Max, you are so right."

Swaying in response to the curves in the road Max sighed and rolled his eyes. "There it is again. Gee, I never get tired of hearing that. It sounds so good rolling off your tongue."

Jane laughed at his exaggerated expression. "You're just heady with all your new-found freedom. You know, if you're too cheeky, I could just as easily take you back to the vet's and tell them you're not acting right and ask if they could keep you a couple more days just to be sure."

"Ah, but you won't. I know you too well. You could never be that cruel."

Jane shot him a cutting glance in the rearview mirror. "No, you're right again, I wouldn't." She cleared her throat and began again. "As I was saying, I'm beginning to understand that it all starts with the way we handle our personal lives. If we understand how life works and know the tools to use to achieve our success—and by that I mean work in our purpose—stay authentic and make good choices, then the whole thing can be used again and again in any situation. There aren't any separate rules for relationships or business. Our personal lives can be overlaid on any aspect of life, and if we use the same methods, we'll achieve what we want."

"It pains me to say this," Max smiled, "but you're right, Jane..."

Jane let out a whoop. "Wow...that musta hurt!"

"Actually, not at all; *you are right*. Since the true measure of greatness is how much greatness you inspire in others, I consider it a privilege to say that. No, really, all it takes is just one person to call their leaders or circulate one petition to force an industry to come to terms with its waste. If one person used a little less energy and then another followed suit, it would become a movement."

Max gazed out the car windows as he spoke. "Humans think of their lives in different aspects. That's true...they have faces and personalities for each. They act and talk one way at home, a different way with the person they love, their children or their pets. There is one language for friends and another for strangers and still another one when they are working. It's not necessary. Your life isn't sectioned off into compartments but rather is a continuous flow of who you are. This too is part of the oneness—designing your life so it becomes united, consistently authentic and uniquely you."

Jane shook her head in agreement. "I think we are limited by our ignorance of what the oneness means and how it works. We humans tend to see ourselves not as another species sharing the planet with animals and plants, but as individuals—beings separate from it, as if that could ever happen. I also think if humans understood the concept of oneness and had the clues I've been given, things would be very different."

Max shook his head in agreement. "I believe that's true. But I think humans also limit themselves in the way they see themselves as compared to others. It's like this huge competition...for everything. The ones that don't have as much as the next feel small and insignificant. The ones that have more stuff feel powerful. Truth is—there are none greater than the next and none smaller. If you only knew how wonderful your species is, what grand deeds you are capable of—besides the ability to accumulate things...Stuff doesn't measure who you truly are and it can't define the soul. It's how you define yourself that allows you to become small and insignificant."

"Well said, Max. This conversation reminds me of the story you told about how the dog got to be man's best friend. The first dog may have jumped the gorge that day to try to remind man of what he was losing, but he also carried the memory of the loss and kept it safe. The natural world knows all mankind has forgotten and remembers it for them. How I wish everyone could have the experience I am having."

"And they could, Jane, if they just asked and listened, it's all still there for them. It would be freely given."

As Jane rounded the last curve before the cabin she changed the subject. "That reminds me of something I wanted to ask you. I never thought about it till the whole vet experience came up. Can anyone else hear us when we speak to each other?"

"No, not unless they are fully awake and aware of the world around them, and that's a choice. They could hear you speak to me, but when they heard me, it would sound like a disjointed bunch of grunts and whines."

"So you can speak to me when others are around and they won't notice?"

"The only time they would notice is when you began to have a long drawn-out conversation with your dog. That might tend to catch someone's attention."

As the cabin came into view, both were laughing—Max with his doggy snorts and Jane's full-bodied joy bubbling out of her. In that moment, life was perfect, a taste of what they had both dreamed possible.

"Boy, am I glad to be home. I'm hungry, and kennel chow isn't like home cookin'. I especially miss the bones."

"Well, you're in luck, there're still a couple more in the freezer and if you're really good...."

Before the conversation could go any deeper they pulled into the driveway and Max let out a deep-throated growl. A flashy silver sports car was parked close to the house; leaning against it was a man who looked totally uncomfortable and foreign. "Who's that?"

"It's Dan," Jane answered in a flat voice.

NINETEEN

...this is my life and no one else will cry my tears if I fail to live it on my own terms

Jane pulled the SUV to a stop, her eyes meeting Dan's. His expression was a mixture of relief and aggravation. It was so like Dan; he hated to be ignored. When she failed to respond to his phone calls, she should have known he would show up.

Slowly opening the car door, Jane took in a deep breath. This was it—the confrontation she knew had been coming for a while. She would rather have had this discussion over the phone, but perhaps it was better to do it in person.

Jane kept her eyes on him as she exited the car. *God, he's handsome.* At six feet, dressed in designer-label clothes and a fifty-dollar haircut, Dan looked very much the young corporate lion he was. Blonde-haired, blue-eyed and fit, he was the poster boy for the American Dream. *What are you doing, Jane? Any woman would die to be on his arm and you're about to toss him to the curb.*

Jane masked her uncertainty with a weak smile. "Hello, Dan, what are you doing here?"

"What do you think I'm doing here?" he responded, annoyed. "You won't answer my messages, and the last time we spoke you were pissed off and told me not to call you again. I'd like to know what's going on and when you're coming back."

"I was mad at you, but I'm not..."

True to his nature, Dan didn't let her finish her sentence. "You were mad at me for wondering when you were coming back. Most girls would take it as a compliment, a sign that I missed you."

"No, Dan, I wasn't upset because you missed me, I was upset because I didn't want to be pressured into coming back. I took a month for a reason. I was angry because I don't want you to fix this for me, I don't need you to fix it. I sure don't need Mitzi Shallowford to fix it for me, and I don't appreciate my problems being a topic for general discussion." A red flush began to creep up Jane's neck as she opened the back of the SUV.

The tenor and pitch of Dan's voice went up an octave. "Hey, Mitzi is a nice gal. I saw her at a club one night, and she asked where you were. I mentioned your little escape to the mountains and that you'd been laid off. That's when she told me about the opening at her press. I wasn't trying to fix it for you; I was just giving you options."

The back hatch now fully open, Dan and Max came face to face. Head lowered and hackles up, a warning growl escaped Max's throat.

"What the hell?" Startled by the dog, Dan backed away from the SUV.

"It's alright, Max," Jane said calmly. "He's mad at me but he's harmless. Dan, this is Max, my dog. Max, this is Dan."

"*Your dog*...What the hell are you thinking, Jane, picking up some stray? You know the apartment complex doesn't allow dogs. What are you going to do with him?"

"Yes, he's my dog. Do me a favor and help me get him out of the car. Just gently grab him under his belly near his back legs, I'll take the front." Max allowed Dan to help get him out of the car; once out, he walked stiff-legged towards the porch.

"Great, now I have dog hair all over my sweater. If you can't get him out by yourself, how did you get him in?"

"Well, usually he gets in under his own steam, but he was bitten by a rattlesnake yesterday. I just picked him up from the vet's and the assistant helped me."

"Rattlesnake?" Dan looked nervously at the ground around him. "Jane, are you insane? Do you hear yourself? Doesn't it bother you to live up here, out in the middle of nowhere with rattlesnakes?"

Jane grabbed Max's new bed and headed for the front porch. "No, I love it and the rattlesnake bite didn't happen here. We were hiking out in the woods. Let me get him settled inside and then you and I need to talk."

"You bet we need to talk!"

Jane opened the front door and she and Max went inside. She laid the bed near the fireplace close to the dining area. Climbing on it, Max looked at her with worry in his eyes. "Jane, I would feel better if you left the door open. I know you say he's harmless, but I am sensing he is quite angry with you. He doesn't trust me and frankly, I don't trust him."

"Okay Max, whatever you want, but honestly, he's all bark and no bite. I'm probably gonna be a few minutes so have a rest." With that she left the cabin, leaving the front door open a crack as Max requested. His hands jammed in his pockets, Dan paced a few feet away from the porch steps.

"Look, Dan, this is not how I want this discussion to go. I don't want to fight with you. I've come to a few decisions, and if we could calmly discuss them that would be great."

"Decisions?" Dan looked at her point-blank. "Decisions from the lady that only two weeks ago couldn't make up her mind about where she wanted to eat on Friday night?"

Jane's feet began to shuffle nervously. This was exactly what she was hoping to avoid. All their arguments always seemed to go like this, Dan on the attack and she on the defensive. She spent most of the time defending her actions rather than stating her case. Dan was a steamroller.

"Well, I suppose that's a fair statement. But Dan, I always had preferences, I just never voiced them and that's my fault. To me, it seemed you had already decided where we should go and I guess I never wanted to disappoint you. You were always so sure of what you wanted and I wasn't sure of anything. That's why I needed this time away from you—away from everything. To make sure I was living my life and not just accompanying you through yours."

"I don't understand."

Jane released the tension in her shoulders and softened her voice. "I know you don't. It may have seemed like I wanted everything you want, but I don't. I don't like the city; I didn't like my job or the direction I seemed to be headed. I wasn't getting any answers caught up in that life. I just had to stop for a while and look at it from a distance."

Dan's eyed widened. "So what are you saying?"

"I'm saying we want different things. That in itself is okay, no two people are alike, but we want *fundamentally* different things. So much so, neither of us would be happy in the life the other wanted. I want to live here; you could never be happy here. What I consider successful isn't what you consider successful. I like the simple quiet life and you love the glitz and the glam of the city, so no matter where we lived, one of us would be unhappy."

"Oh my God…you're breaking up with me? I drove three hours so you could break up with me?"

"Yes, Dan, I am. It's the only way I see—"

"Want me to tell you what I see, Jane? I see a woman that's making the biggest mistake of her life. Atlanta has all the intellectual and cultural stimulation you could ever want, and quiet or not, you're a pretty intellectual person. Where are you going to find that stuck up here with nothing but trees and hillbillies? I bet if you put this whole town in one room the combined IQ would still be under eighty."

"That's not fair, Dan—you sound like a snob. This town is great and so are the people in it. Maybe some haven't gone to college, but they have a mighty wisdom of their own."

"Oh, I bet. That ought to come in handy if your pig is sick or your carburetor goes out." Pacing again, Dan unleashed a passionate diatribe. "Listen to me, Jane; you're all stressed out over losing your job. You're not thinking clearly. I'll admit I haven't been very comforting or supportive about all of this, but I thought you'd use your logic and just find another job—it's no big deal. Dumping me and moving away isn't going to solve your problems, it's just running away from them. Tomorrow morning you're still going to need a job, and what are you going to do here?"

Now it was Jane's turn to tuck her hands in the pockets of her jeans. She felt herself shrinking as she tried to explain her choices. "Dan, you know I have always wanted to write—books, not news stories. I thought I might get a job as a waitress, anything to pay the bills and give me the time to work on something substantial."

"A waitress," Dan spat the words. "That's rich. A four-year degree so you can serve home cooking at some roadside diner. Come on, Jane. Look, if you want to work as a waitress and write, come back to Atlanta and at least get a job in a high-end restaurant where you'll make decent tips."

"Oh, now it's okay—me wanting to write. You never seemed happy about that before," Jane snapped.

"Well, that's because I didn't think you were serious. I thought it was just some pie-in-the-sky-someday kind of dream. Other than the newspaper, I've never read anything you've ever written, so how seriously could I take you?"

Jane walked past Dan and leaned against his car. He was right. She'd never written anything. He was throwing the big guns at her, and she was paying the price for her past inability to assert who she really was. As angry as he was, he was making some good points. *Maybe he's right, maybe I am reacting to the lay-off and I would be better off in Atlanta till I get all of this sorted.* Jane felt her resolve wavering. *It certainly would be easier on me if he and I were together, sharing expenses instead of shouldering all the bills myself. I never let him see the real me. Maybe if I had, we wouldn't be here right now. Maybe if I stood up for myself more, voiced my preferences once in a while, our relationship would be okay—good even…*

Dan could see Jane deliberating and moved in for the kill. His voice honeyed. "Jane, sweetie, if you want to write, then write. I'll take care of you while you give it a try. If we leave right now, we can drop the mutt at the local humane society and be back in Atlanta in time for a couple of glasses of wine and some great pasta at Salvano's. We can talk all this out and celebrate a new beginning. Things will be better, you'll see."

The condescending tone of his voice ran all over Jane. She stuffed her hands deeper into her pockets, and as she did the knuckles of her left hand bumped something hard. Unclenching her fist she fingered the object. It was the acorn Grandfather Oak had placed in her hand only days ago. Short clips of conversations rushed to the front of her mind. *Potential...the patterns of your life...plant your seed in fertile ground...only you can create who you are...authentic.* She pulled the seed into the palm of her hand and squeezed it. Jacob's words rang in her ears. *Fear and doubt fight within you; the one that wins is the one you feed.* Dan was feeding her doubt and, once again, she was allowing someone else to sway her.

Closing her eyes, she dropped her awareness from her head to her heart. *How do I feel about this?* Her mind's camera showed her a little movie of her and Dan back in Atlanta, back in the life they had shared. She felt sad and smothered; she had chosen the dead-end path. *How do I feel about staying here?* The scene in her head changed and she saw herself beside the fireplace with Max on a cold rainy night. Despite the weather, she felt peace, happiness and an autonomy that filled her with excitement. As her prospects showed themselves, her pulse quickened, and with it, resolve flowed back into her veins.

This is my life and no one else will cry my tears if I fail to live it on my own terms. Dan's management techniques would have worked on the old Jane. Devaluing her own wisdom, she would have adopted his, yet the Jane she was discovering with Max trusted her own judgment.

Max—the callous way Dan referred to Max gripped her chest. The thought of breaking her promise or leaving him behind made her stomach churn and left a metallic taste on her tongue. Even the hint of betraying all that she had promised him felt like poison in her mouth. He was part of her, she loved him, and she would never give him up.

Straightening her spine, Jane turned back to Dan and locked her eyes on his.

"I don't want anyone to take care of me while I *try* to write. I'm not some hot-house plant or piece of fine art. I want my own voice; I want to make my own mark in the world. And for your information,

Max may be a mutt, but he has taught me more than anything or anyone ever has. He's saved my life in more ways than one, and he's not going anywhere.

"Dan, you're a great guy and someday you'll make a great partner for some lucky girl, but that girl's not me. You and I won't work. If I go back with you, I'll just fall into the same stagnant pattern and wither away on the vine. I've enjoyed our time together, but that life doesn't serve me anymore. I'm staying. I'll come down next weekend and clear out my stuff."

Dan sucked in a deep breath and glared, "Okay, but you're losing the best thing you've ever had—you know that, don't you?" He scanned her face for any sign of cracks in her determination. Finding none, he threw his hands in the air and stalked off towards his car. "Do what you want, but when this blows up in your face, don't come running to me."

Jane walked to the porch as his engine revved. She turned to watch him go down the driveway and point his car towards Atlanta. When his taillights vanished from view, a weight lifted from her and the ever-present headache ceased. Jane touched her forehead. She knew this choice had been lingering for too long and her body had paid the price.

She had held her conflict tightly knotted inside her head. Now that the last die was cast, the dis-ease unwound itself and slipped away.

For better or for worse, she had made her choice and finally stood up for the Jane she knew herself to be. Instead of an ending, the moment was a new beginning. Pushing open the door, she was light and excited about her decision.

"Is he gone?" Max lifted his head from his paws.

"Yes, he's gone. It's done and I'm staying."

Jane watched as the tension drained from Max's body. She knew he'd been holding his breath, hoping for the best, but knowing the worst was a possibility. As hard as the conversation between her and Dan had been, she knew in those minutes that Max was living a fresh hell of his own. Imagining himself alone again, cast off, he had only his faith in her to carry him.

"You didn't think I would leave you and go back, did you?" she asked as she sat down in front of her laptop.

"I'll admit I had my moments."

"I meant what I said, Max. You're home with me now. This is home."

Max laid his head down and sighed. He watched silently as she lifted the top of her computer. "What are you doing now? That's the first time since you've been here I've seen you sit there."

"Max, I've been thinking a lot about what I want to write. Before I picked you up today I had a talk with an ant that told me about meaning. He said finding your purpose was great, but when you use it in a way that brings meaning to it, you discover the secret of living."

Jane twisted in her chair to face the dog. "We both know it was no accident I fell on those steps. Chance played no part in opening the door to these experiences. All the parts and pieces of my life have been conspiring to bring me to this exact place in time.

"Even my name—I used to hate my name and all the stupid nicknames my classmates came up with to torture me, like plain Jane or Jane Doe. Now, and bear with me here, I may be fishing too deeply, but I see how perfect my name really is. *I am Jane Doe.* I'm every woman or any man. How many thousands of people do you think ask the same questions I asked? How many people are living lives of quiet discontent, secretly longing for some sort of meaning that will make sense out of their existence? I believe there are thousands of human beings that lose their way and can't figure out where their path begins or ends, just like me."

Gesturing passionately, Jane continued. "It's no coincidence I'm a writer, either. What has been given to me is an experience that can be translated and given to anyone who cares to listen. The night I spent at the Council of Animals, with White Bear, broke my heart. I told him I would help them, even though at the time I didn't know how. Now I believe I can use my purpose, my gift as a writer, to do just that."

Jane plucked a few keys on the keyboard and a blank page opened on the screen. "What if people knew everything I've learned? What if they could travel with me and experience everything I have experienced—you, Grandmother Spider, White Bear, even the Great Snake. If I can use my talent to take them on this journey with me, let them hear their voices as they tell their stories, it may cause them to understand how life works and how easy it is to be who you are. Maybe it would resonate with them. If others knew Creator left a blueprint for living in the natural world, would they be so quick to ignore it or destroy it? I think not. Max, even if just one person got it, that would bring meaning to my purpose *and* my life."

"So you're going to write our story?"

"Yes, I am." Jane's eyes sparkled as she flashed a big grin to Max. "Only the names will be changed to protect the innocent."

"Do you think anyone will believe you?"

"I'll write it as fiction—it's easier to suspend your beliefs if you're being told a story. Some will take it as fiction; some may just think it's a nice story but a crock of crap. But a few will consider the possibility and maybe—just maybe—it will touch something, open a door. All it takes is just a small sliver of light. For those few, that light may lead them to the conclusion that while we search for things that will bring meaning to our lives, the big secret is, life can't bring meaning to you—you bring meaning to life."

Jane threw her hands up in the air and turned back to the laptop. "It doesn't matter whether they think it's true or not, I can still jam a lot of wisdom on the pages." She chuckled. "If I were half as good a student about the nature of love as I am about the nature of life, things would be dandy."

"That's another chapter, Jane, and it will come. Self first and when you're centered and ready to bring all your gifts to a relationship, you'll know it."

"I'll take that as a promise, Max. The only thing I ask is next time we leave out rattlesnakes or anything poisonous."

Max snorted and shut his eyes. Few things were better than a good nap, and if Jane was going to write, he would have ample opportunity to catch forty winks. Smiling, he silently congratulated himself on a job well done. He marveled at the natural order of things and how, when you're in harmony with the flow, everything works out as if by magic. Jane had found her purpose and meaning, and he had guided her to all the lessons she needed to anchor that in her life. He was living his promise, the same promise the first dog made long ago. True to that purpose, he had led Jane home.

The keys on the laptop clicked away furiously as Jane began to fill the page with words.

Chapter One

Lying on the wet steps, Laura had no idea how long she had been unconscious, or for that matter, where she was. All she knew was it was dark, she had a large bleeding bump on her forehead, and she was soaked to the bone...

We invite you to have the following peek at the first chapter of the sequel to *Strays,* as yet untitled.

ONE

Jane winced as the thunder broke against the roof of her cabin. It must be directly overhead, she thought as the windows shivered in their casings. The storm was bad, the worst she had seen since she'd taken up residence in the Smokies over a year ago.

It was a terrible day to paint, too humid for it to dry quickly, but she was stir crazy. It had been raining heavily off and on for hours and the electricity failed some time ago, so her new PC was as useless as the TV. She had to do something, and painting her office seemed like the only option.

The sound roared down the valley like the angry growl of some enormous celestial beast. It ricocheted off the mountainsides, bouncing from one to another, pushed east toward the flatlands by a fierce wind that tore at the trees. Jane laid her paint roller back in its tin pan and walked to the window, glancing over at Max as she went. He was sleeping peacefully in the far corner of the room. Sprawled on the drop cloth, he showed no concern for the tempest outside. Lying on his back, his legs splayed to either side, he was content to let the storm pass without his attention.

Thunder didn't bother her—in fact, she thought of it as the

Creator's voice, awesome and powerful, reminding her that He was ever present. She welcomed thundershowers and the slow bold sound they brought with them. But the wind was another story. Jane liked a good breeze, but strong winds made her restless and nervous. The wildness of them seemed to blow through her body and take control of her nervous system, compelling her to pace and roam, the wind matching its own aversion for stillness against her love of peace.

Jane pressed her forehead against the glass. It was more like night than day outside, and she could barely focus on the trees through the blur of the watery window. She could feel the force of the rain splattering against the pane, sharp and wet. Lightning flickered constantly, illuminating the squall every other second. *Bless anyone out in this; I'm glad I'm not out on the road somewhere.*

Twigs and shredded leaves flew past her, driven sideways in a straight line, so it should not have come as a shock when a small branch rebounded off the windowsill. But she jerked back startled, squealing in surprise. At once Max was on high alert. In one swift move he was standing, head down, ears rigid and straining. His once-open mouth was tightly shut and he seemed to be holding his breath, lest it interfere with his ability to hear.

A short low growl escaped him, and in the next second he was barking wildly, scrambling towards the door, hindered by drop cloth and hardwood floor.

"Max, it's okay! I'm okay," Jane said, stunned by his intensity. He was out of the room before she could finish her sentence. She hurried to follow him down the hall, his frantic barking ringing in her ears. By the time she reached him, he was digging madly at the front door. "What is it, Max? What's out there? You can't go out there, honey, it's dangerous. It's just a storm, Max, that's all." But her words fell on deaf ears. He had one goal in mind—to get out that door—and he didn't have time to translate the reason into language.

Maneuvering her way around the frenzied dog, Jane finally managed to turn the knob. At a dead run, Max flew off the porch and into the teeth of the gale. Already the mist that gave the Smoky Mountains their name was seeping up from the ground, and Jane lost sight of Max in just a few short seconds. Her only compass was the sound of his snarls and yowls, and when they ceased her knuckles whitened as she gripped the door frame.

Rain and wind swirled under the porch roof, wetting the front of her T shirt. Jane stood motionless, laboring to catch his voice amidst the thunder. Time stood still as she waited for Max to reappear. She tasted panic as her throat began to constrict.

The past year had cemented their relationship. She had written her book, the tale of her time in the mountains, meeting Max and the strange journey both had taken. Max would listen as she read chapters to him, adding ideas, correcting when necessary, but always being encouraging and supportive.

They celebrated each step of the process together, from submitting the manuscript to finding an agent and finally publishing the book. Her advance was large enough to buy the option on the cabin with enough left over to begin the remodeling she'd dreamed about for so long. He was as proud of her as she was of herself for grabbing life by the throat and making her dreams her reality. They had created a life together, had a home…became a family.

Their love for each other was as real and close as any relationship between humans ever was. It was hard to explain that—the intensity of it, the loyalty involved—to someone who didn't have an animal companion. But whether four-legged, winged, finned, or legless, these beloveds claimed a place in the heart as strong as any person could ever hold.

It was a bond that didn't depend on how much money you made or what social circles you ran in. It didn't matter if you were educated or even had a job. How attractive you were wasn't an issue, and where you lived was of no consequence. No, when these companions looked at you, it was always with eyes that said they thought you hung the moon at night and called forth the sun every day. No matter who you were or what your circumstances, they asked only one thing: to lie at your feet or curl up in your lap and just share life with you. They kept your secrets, bore your tears, and even on a bad day there was always forgiveness and steady unconditional love.

Jane wrapped her arms around her ribs as she ventured near the edge of the porch. She scanned the yard looking for any sign of Max. The ground was saturated, and pools of water stood in the driveway. The ditch down by the road ran to overflowing with muddy churning water, feral and dangerous. Just when she tensed to leap to the ground and look for him, Max appeared, trotting towards her, carrying something small and grey in his mouth. He didn't stop or even look at her as he hurried through the open door to the living room.

Jane followed him inside. He was standing beside his doggy bed, licking furiously at the tiny grey mass. The cabin was so gloomy and dark from the storm, it wasn't until she knelt beside him that she recognized the lump to be a kitten. Lying on its side, the teeny cat was still—its eyes shut tight, a little pink tongue lolling out of a miniature mouth. The poor thing was so wet that its fur clung to its body, giving it a skeletal appearance. Jane didn't know how old the kitten was, but it couldn't have been more than a few weeks, a month at best.

"Oh my God, Max, a kitten!" Jane gasped. "Is it alive?"

Max stopped his licking long enough to clip out an answer. "I don't know, I think so…. It was when I found it. It's so cold…. I can't tell if it's still breathing."

Jane jumped up and ran down the hall to the bathroom. She fumbled beneath the sink, rifling through the contents of the cabinet until she found the hot water bottle. After waiting for the tap water to warm, she filled it half full, grabbed a towel and ran back to the living room.

"Here, let's get it warm," Jane said. Max let her carefully scoop the kitten onto the towel covering the water bottle before continuing his ministrations. Seconds later, the tiny cat gagged, water spewing from its nose and mouth, and it dragged in a ragged breath. Its little eyes flickered open as it retched water from its lungs. Both Max and Jane inhaled deeply, as if doing so would help the creature continue drawing air on its own.

"Max, how did you know?"

"I heard it. You woke me when you startled, and I heard it screeching through the storm," Max said as he watched the kitten fight to clear its airway. "For something so small, it sure has a voice. I found it in the ditch, clinging to the branch of a bush. There were two others...but they were dead already."

"Awww...poor things. Are you sure, Max, sure they were gone?"

"Yes, I'm sure."

"How did they get there? Where did they come from?" Jane asked sadly.

"I don't know—abandoned maybe—or maybe their mother had them in the culvert, a stray herself."

"What'll we do now?"

"I don't know. Wait, I guess, to see if it's going to live." Max began to lick the tiny cat again, encouraging it to move around, willing it back to life.

Several long minutes passed as they both stared intently at the cat. Their attention was rewarded when the kitten struggled to right itself, coughing and sputtering the last of the water out of its diminutive body. Pulling to its feet, the kitten staggered and lurched off the water bottle and headed straight for Max. Still wet and panic-stricken, it extended minuscule translucent claws and tried to climb the fur on Max's chest. Jane laughed out loud at the sound of its first terrified mewl. Eyes wide as saucers, Max held very still as the kitten, still too weak to climb, dropped between his legs and then burrowed against him.

"It doesn't like the water bottle—seems it prefers your warmth, Max," Jane smiled. For all Max's objections to cats, he didn't seem to mind this kitten's advances.

"Well, that makes sense," Max replied sheepishly. "It's a smart kitty that knows natural body warmth is better than a substitute."

"A smart kitty?" Jane was beginning to enjoy this. "I've never heard you use 'smart' and 'kitty' in the same sentence. As a matter of fact, I seem to recall you having a distinct dislike for felines."

Max pretended not to hear her as he licked the kitten and then nosed it into the crook between his leg and his chest. Only a speck of grey remained as the kitten settled into the dog's long hair.

"Poor thing is shivering."

Jane wasn't about to let Max change the subject. "I'm surprised at you, Max. For as much as you kidded around about cats and your declared distaste for their company, I'm shocked that you bothered to rescue our little friend."

Max's eyes turned serious as he looked at her. "It was another living thing in trouble. I may dislike cats, but if I can make a difference between life and death, I don't hesitate. It's what dogs do—how we are—especially with baby animals. We can be quite protective, you know. And even though I joke about it, cats have their place too—though they tend to be a bit arrogant, which I guess is natural considering their nickname."

"What's their nickname?"

"God's glove…. Didn't I ever tell you that story?"

"No. With all the stories and lessons I've learned, you never offered one up about cats…and the subject came up enough. Tell me, please."

"Okay." Max looked down to check on his little ward and then began. "Many years ago, there was a winter that was particularly deep and hard. The cold was so bitter and the snow so deep there was little food to be found for either man or beast. It was especially hard for one old woman who lived on the edge of a small settlement. The old woman was a widow, and although she planted and toiled in her garden all summer, the harvest was meager and just enough to get her through till spring.

"The woman was careful with her stores and rationed out her grains and vegetables to be sure she wouldn't run out before the ground warmed enough to welcome new seed. There would be just enough, but she couldn't afford any waste or spoilage. But as life often does, it sent her a problem she hadn't allowed for.

"Because the winter was so hard, the mice and rats of the meadows could not find much to eat. They foraged here and scurried there in search of food, and it wasn't long until they discovered the old widow's stores. The unwelcome rodents tried everything they could to steal away bits of grain, and the old woman tried everything she knew to keep them away.

"The battle for survival was constant. Each day she would notice a new hole gnawed in her modest cabin and made repairs. Each night the mice gnawed another way in. Before long the widow became tired and worn from the fight.

"One night while the widow wearily sat guarding her food, there came a knock at the door. She opened it to find a tall broad man at the door, almost frozen to the core. He was nearly blue from the cold, and his long hair and beard were stiff with ice.

"The old woman took great pity on the stranger and ushered him in, seating him by the small fireplace. After he took some time to warm, the woman offered him a bowl of hot stew and a piece of bread. While she knew she would soon not have enough food to get through the winter, she would not refuse to share what she did have.

"All the while the great man ate, the sound of tiny scratching and gnawing could be heard. When at last he asked her where the sound was coming from, the woman burst into tears and told the man of her struggle with the mice and rats.

"The man stood up and said, 'Woman, you have welcomed me to your home, warmed and fed me, and you shall be rewarded.'

"With that, he took his glove and threw it on the floor. Slowly the fingers became legs and the thumb became a tail. In just a few moments the glove had taken life and became the first cat.

"No sooner than the cat took its first breath, the scratching and gnawing attracted him and he sprung into action. He began to hunt the rodents with great speed and cunning, and long before the man left the cabin the mice and rats were killed and the old woman's food was safe.

"The woman's unselfish act had been rewarded by the stranger, and the first cat had come to be. Who the night visitor was and where he came from was never settled. But in many parts of this land, the cat is called God's Glove and the story goes that the animal is so favored by Creator, He imbued the cat with nine lives instead of just one."

"Wow, Max, that's lovely," Jane said as he finished the story. "It reminds me of the passage in the Bible that talks about entertaining angels unawares."

"Yeah, well, I don't know about angels, but cats take the whole 'favored by Creator' thing to the limit. Sometimes they are social and sometimes they act like the gift the legend makes them out to be—gets on my nerves."

"Your nerves don't seem to be too bothered at the moment," Jane smiled as she motioned towards the ball of fur curled up next to him.

Max looked down just as the kitten began to mew again in earnest. Not responding to Jane's last barb he said, "I think it's hungry."

"What are we going to feed it, Max? It looks way too young for cow's milk." Jane raised herself off the floor enough to peek out the window. They had lost track of the weather during the drama of the rescue and revival of the kitten. "I know—the storm is about over and we can go to the Feed and Seed. Dub will fix us up, no doubt." Jane stood up and started for the kitchen. "I'll get my keys. You can put kitty on the water bottle…. That should keep it warm till we get back."

Max looked at her with hesitation in his eyes. "If you don't mind, could you go alone? I don't think I should leave the little guy just yet."

Jane's mouth dropped open. "You're giving up a ride in the car to stay home with a cat?"

"Well, I plucked it from the jaws of death. I feel a certain responsibility to see its recovery through, and I don't happen to think *now* is the best time to leave it alone."

Jane stood for a moment, grinning widely at Max. When he could no longer stand the heat of her scrutiny, he turned away and laid his head on his leg, careful not to crush the kitten. Jane kept on grinning as she grabbed her keys and donned her rain slicker. She had never known Max to be wrong about anything and did not doubt his opinions. *That kitten might just as well have crawled through the skin on his chest straight into his heart. He's hooked.* She supposed the wisest among us still had lessons to learn and walls to break down, and Max had just pulled his next lesson from the muddy water of a ditch.

He would have to recant his judgment and overcome his own baggage in this new relationship with the kitten. *Ought to be interesting,* she thought. *This time I get to watch the lesson as it unfolds instead of living it myself.*

Opting to leave by the front door, she called back over her shoulder, "I'll be back shortly; you take care of our little charge while I'm gone…Mama." She heard Max's disgusted snort in reply to the mama comment as she shut the door. *Yes indeed, this could get very interesting.*

Jeanne Webster, CPC

Jeanne Webster is a certified professional life coach that niches in teen/young adult issues, life transitions and spiritual integration. She is an award-winning author, speaker and columnist.

Her first book, *If You Could Be Anything, What Would You Be?*, is a life mapping guidebook for teens that connects the dots between education and life goals. *If You Could Be Anything* won two national awards, the iParenting Award and the U.S.A. Book Awards for best book of 2004 in the teen/young adult category. It is used in schools and mentor programs throughout the country. It is also reprinted internationally.

Ms. Webster has worked with the Future Business Leaders of America and the Character Education Partnership in Washington D.C. In 2007 she was contracted by Neale Donald Walsch's School of the New Spirituality to write a guidebook for Mr. Walsch's bestseller, *Conversations with God for Teens.* She was a workshop leader and on staff with SNS for more than two years as well as coaching in her private practice.

Jeanne also worked as a life skills coach with domestic violence survivors and as a court-appointed coach working with parent/child reunification cases in her county's court system.

The subject of numerous articles, Ms. Webster has been interviewed on more than 85 radio talk shows throughout the country. *Strays* is her third book and first fiction.